VIGILANTE VENGEANCE

"Keep your hands away from your gunbelts." John Lieninger stepped into the street aiming a twelve gauge side-by-side at Moses' and Mudeater's heads. "You know these scatter-guns have a wide spread, so both of you be smart and don't do anything except stand still." He whistled and two dozen masked men emerged from the surrounding shadows like wraiths from a bone orchard fog. All brought rifles. One carried a rope under one arm.

"You might want to reconsider this, John."

"Keep quiet, Jeb, until we attend to this Sioux."

Mudeater, who had slitted his eyes and appeared to be sleeping on his feet, perked to life.

One masked man cocked his rifle and leveled it at Mudeater's left ear. *"String him up!"*

BUSHWHACKERS

STEVEN PHILIP JONES

LEISURE BOOKS NEW YORK CITY

To Lisa and Katie,
For all your patience and faith,
I love you with all my heart.

A LEISURE BOOK®

August 2006

Published by

Dorchester Publishing Co., Inc.
200 Madison Avenue
New York, NY 10016

ISBN 0-8439-5717-4

Printed in the United States of America.

BUSHWHACKERS

Columbine, Columbine
Blue in the Rockies
Will you miss me, when I've gone away?
—Bill Fries and Chip Davis, "Columbine"

CHAPTER ONE

The sheriff, Jeb Moses, borrowed a buckboard and tandem from the livery to retrieve the body. He handed the reins to his deputy, Ted Coleman, opting to escort the wagon riding his old paint, King Charles.

"This is one of them moments God made deputies for, Teddy."

Coleman smiled and shrugged. He knew his boss, almost twenty years older, no longer appreciated the trauma a pair of rusty spring shocks and three miles of petrified ruts and chuckholes could inflict on a pair of kidneys. Happened to anyone who lived long enough.

The lawmen spotted the body laying where the old prospector Connie had promised they would, by the side of the wagon trail bridging Eleanor with the foothills of the San Juan's second-tier elevations.

"Would've been nice if Connie had just

strapped the poor buzzard to his mule," Moses groused.

"He's scared of dead folks. Some people are that way. Afraid a corpse will jump up and bite them if they touch it."

Moses snorted. "If he thinks that, then Connie's mule is smarter than he is."

"It's got nothing to do with smarts. It's a feeling. The way some people get when they're in a cave and they feel like the walls are closing in on top of them. They go *loco* until they get outside. Folks can't help what they feel, Mose."

"If you think that, Teddy, then Connie's mule is smarter than you too."

It was almost three o'clock, the air clement under the late June sun as blowflies hovered and lighted and hovered over and on the body's head.

"This ought to be pretty." Moses dismounted King Charles. "If we're lucky, whoever he is won't be stinking yet." Moses did not bother ground-tying his paint. Come buffalo stampede or angry posse, King Charles knew to stay put.

Coleman parked the wagon, kicked the brake lever with his left foot, and jumped to the ground. "Good Lord, Mose!" he said. "It's Jon Brand!"

"Aw, no." Moses slouched to one knee for a closer look.

No doubt about it. Jon, who'd turned sixteen in April, was supposed to be attending school in Virginia. His face was older, now more man than boy, and his body was thicker across the chest and shoulders than when they had last seen him in August. Nevertheless, this was Jon Brand.

Coleman asked, "What's he doing out here?"

Jon was dressed in a brown cloth coat and traveling clothes. If he had been wearing a hat it had blown away. A possible bag laid beside Jon, inside which Moses found a capote, a slicker, and what the sheriff estimated was the remains of two or three days' worth of supplies. A Navy Colt revolver was sheathed in its holster on Jon's gunbelt while his right hand clutched a Hawkins rifle.

"My guess," said Moses, "is he rode the train into Lake City or Rawlins Station, then walked the rest of the way home."

"Not quite all the way." Coleman spat.

"Yeah. Pretty obvious he never had a chance."

Moses scattered the blowflies so he could examine a bullet hole bored into Jon's left temple. "Looks like a .40 caliber round made this, like the others." Next he tugged open Jon's soggy blue cotton shirt. "It's here."

Coleman grunted as he scavenged the ground bordering the road. A fair tracker, he could normally be relied upon to sift out a trail, but that day, nothing. "Hang it!" he exclaimed. "They've done it again! Not one track! These bushwhackers must have worn wings and plugged Jon from the clouds!"

"I reckon the shot came from over there." Moses stood and pointed at a low knoll three hundred yards behind Coleman.

"Not one most folks could make."

"You've said that before, Teddy, but it still don't help us none."

During the last three years twenty-six men, women, and children had been murdered throughout the Colorado San Juan range, the majority in or near Moses' jurisdiction—all shot in the head from a distance and all with a tell-tale X carved in their chests. No large parties were ever ambushed—only solitary travelers or groups of two or three—and the killers never left any trail to follow. Even the regional Plains Indian tribes claimed they had not seen so much as a stray track left by the bushwhackers. On the other hand, none of the victims had been Indians, which made many local settlers suspicious that this was the work of Colorow and his band of White River Utes or some renegade Arapahos. Moses doubted it, as did Colonel Adams, the reservation agent over at the Los Pinos Indian Agency. This sort of ambush was not their style.

"So what are you going to tell the Brands?"

"Not much 'cept Jon's dead." Not that Moses did not wish there was more he could tell the Brands. But what? That he would not rest until whoever waylaid Jon was dancing a jig at the end of a rope? That he had always liked Jon, and the Brands could be proud of their son? All true but cold comfort for the young man's parents.

"Mr. Brand isn't going to like this."

"Ciphered that one out for yourself, eh?"

"Oh, you know what I mean, Mose."

Moses knew. Joshua Brand was not a bad man, but, as the owner of the Nox Mining Syndicate, one of the largest employers in southwestern Colorado, Brand was wealthy and powerful. As was the case with a few other wealthy and powerful people with which the sheriff was acquainted, Joshua had a tendency to believe that all men are created equal. The Brands, however, he felt to be a trifle more equal than most.

"Come on," Moses told Coleman. "Let's load Jon into the buckboard and take him home."

CHAPTER TWO

"She sleep now."

Doc Gluzunov, a knarred, lanky Russian old enough to remember Napoleon's Grand Army invading his motherland, lowered his husky voice into a gravelly whisper as he gently shut the door to Ella Brand's bedroom.

"I give her some powder. Barbiturate acid. You let her sleep. No disturb her." Gluzunov patted his faded black physician's bag, emphasizing his authority. "Best thing for her. Shock to her mind . . . horrible. I know. Lost my son, Petr, during war with Turkey in 1854, but ache as fresh today. My condolences, Mr. Brand."

Joshua thanked Gluzunov and led him down to the front door. A minute later Joshua returned to his private study on the first floor where Moses was waiting.

"Please sit, Jeb." The somber chamber was decorated with oak panels, fluted wall columns, six-foot-high round-arched windows with purple velvet drapes, an antique Persian carpet, and frosted glass shades on the oil lamps. Joshua pointed without looking to a pair of cowhide-upholstered chairs in front of the large oak desk.

Moses begged off, self-conscious of the gray trail dirt coating his denim britches. "I'll stand," he said, holding his dusty hat in his thick fingers.

"Suit yourself."

Joshua stepped behind his desk and stood beside his judge's chair to stare out the nearest window. Like his late father Luther, Joshua Brand was of average height and weight with the cultivated features of an educated person, but equipped with the brawny shoulders and scarred hands of someone reared on steady rough work. He was clean-shaven in accordance to Eastern fashions, but, so long as he was at home in Colorado and not receiving visitors from Virginia or some other New England state, Joshua wore his thick gunmetal hair long even in summer.

"Jon was coming home to surprise his mother," Joshua spoke, his tenor one of recitation rather than explanation. "For the Fourth of July. Their favorite holiday. Remember? You definitely lit the fuse to enough firecrackers for him not so long ago. Jon was going to stay until the statehood festival before returning to Virginia. That meant missing the first few days of classes, but the headmaster was a friend of father's. They taught at Patrick Henry together. He understood."

Joshua's gray eyes gazed dully down at the town of Eleanor, named after his wife, the former Ella Kirk. Their home, situated atop a bluff on

Eleanor's northern periphery, provided a commanding view of the town that, in the past, he had found picturesque and balming.

"I gotta ask," Moses interrupted, "why Jon was walking by himself."

Joshua clasped hands behind his back. "You think that was a mistake?"

"I've gotta . . ."

"You must ask questions. It's your job." He paused. "Jon was supposed to arrive from Richmond on the same train with a delivery of smelting supplies. I dispatched men to Rawlins Station yesterday to pick up the order and escort him home. I can only assume he arrived on an earlier train and youthful exuberance got the better of his common sense."

Moses nodded. "I ain't faulting Jon one bit for what happened to him."

"Of course."

"I was fond of Jon, real fond. Listen. I'm sheriff, sworn to uphold the law. And that is what I am going to do when I find these butchers. They'll get their day in front of Judge Berthel. It's just . . . well . . . we both know I used to be a different sort of man, and I'll always be grateful to you for taking a chance on me back then. Maybe that's why part of me would rather string up these curs than round them up."

A hard flame kindled behind Joshua's eyes. "You do what you think is best, Jeb."

Moses decided to drop the subject. "I'd best get along. If you or Ella need anything . . ."

"Thank you, Jeb. For everything."

Alone, for the first time since Moses broke the

news, Joshua was not sure what to do next. There were funeral arrangements to make, but he could not do that without Ella. She would never forgive him if he did; he knew because he would have felt the same way in her place. Joshua could not recall ever missing his wife's company more than that moment, not even during the War, when there was no way of knowing if he would see Ella again or meet his baby boy. Back then it was only the dream of returning home to his new family that had kept Joshua fighting to survive through Five Forks, Gettysburg, and Murfreesboro. Especially Murfreesboro.

Preferring to forget about that part of his life, Joshua recollected Moses and what the sheriff said before leaving: *"We both know I use to be a different sort of man, and I'll always be grateful to you for taking a chance on me back then. Maybe that's why part of me would rather string up these curs than round them up."* He knew Moses liked Jon. He also knew that, for three years, Moses, Deputy Coleman, and a host of lawmen and trackers had failed to pick up so much as a scent of the "cross killers," the name bestowed on the cagey bushwhackers by Colorado journalists. Escaping Moses in particular was no small feat. Even the orneriest prospector had to agree that nobody knew this neck of the Rockies better than Jeb Moses, who, for over a decade, had been *The Scourge of the San Juans,* as one yellowback's title had immortalized him. Moses' career reached a point where turning him into a lawman became the only way to stop him, which is what Joshua did when Moses approached Brand with the suggestion after Eleanor's last sheriff, Art Morris, was killed in the line of duty.

"I'm only scared of two things," Moses had confessed on that day. "Dying young and growing older. Well, I'm getting too old for outlawing, and I can't say it's been as easy for me to sleep at night as it use to. But I figure I'm in my prime when it comes to snaring desperados. I wager the most cocksure rustler will think twice 'fore trying to feed on my range."

Joshua was not a betting man by nature, and he knew hiring Moses was a gamble. For six years, though, Eleanor had been one of the most peaceful towns in the Rockies thanks to Moses; but the cross killers were proving better than him again and again. The bushwhackers had roamed free for three years, and now Jon was dead.

Something had to be done.

"Oh, I'm going crazy cooped up in here!"

He called for Juanita, the housemaid. She did her best to hide that she had been crying as Joshua instructed her to check in on Mrs. Brand from time to time until his return. "I must get some air," he explained to her in Spanish. "I can't say how long I'll be gone."

"*Si, Señor* Brand. *Haré así.*"

Walking towards the horse barn, Joshua's attention was attracted to his lone neighbor on the bluff, a boarded-up Victorian built by Amos Kirk, his father-in-law and Luther Brand's former best friend and partner. Except for the degree of upkeep, the place was a twin of the Brands' Victorian. The Brands' grounds were pampered and manicured, the gardens tended and blooming, with the house sporting a fresh coat of paint, chestnut brown with yellow and green, gingerbread and scarlet trim. The lawn of the Kirks' whilom mansion was a court of tangled witch grass and wildflowers, while the house, empty for fourteen years, had had its clapboards and shutters pecked clean of paint by the Rocky Mountain winters. Untended, it was left to fade toward a cancerous gray under the Colorado summer sun.

This was the first time Joshua could recollect scrutinizing the neighboring Victorian on anything more than a superficial level since his wife had ordered it boarded up in 1865, the day after Amos was hanged for killing Luther. The Brands had considered demolishing it then, but never got around to it, instead falling into the habit of ignoring it. Now something about the gray place seemed to be beckoning Joshua to walk up the cracked, crumbling front path, the warped rickety steps, and on to the dilapidated veranda where the old swing hung until the day Amos tore it down.

"Blast you, you witless old fussbudget."

Joshua Brand was not a God-fearing man. Not since the War. In spite of that he liked to think that Jon was in heaven, and, if there was a heaven for Jon, Joshua prayed there was also a hell for Amos Kirk. However, looking at the Kirk mansion did give Joshua an idea. A desperate idea, but something he could try nonetheless.

Joshua cinched his saddle on Parbuckle, his blanket Appaloosa stallion. Stepping into the left stirrup, he swung himself into the saddle and galloped out of the barn. As he headed down the bluff, Joshua surveyed Eleanor again.

The town, founded by Luther and Amos in 1849, prospered at 11,400 feet above sea level, sheltered in the eastern edge of an amphitheater rimmed by lolling piedmonts and kaleidoscopic cliffs along the western lee of the Great Divide. From here Joshua could see Tansey Creek dividing Eleanor in halves before it took its twining leave through the combering tableland that spread out like a Chinese fan on the other side of town. Huge cottonwoods lined the wooden sidewalks of every street east and west of the Tansey; only the main street, Argos Avenue, ran through both sections, thanks to a covered bridge at the creek's narrowest point. Rising along Eleanor's southern perimeter was a pair of high graceful hills, behind which ascended the steeple of St. Wenceslaus' Catholic Church. The hills obstructed everything beneath the steeple, including St. Wenceslaus' churchyard, the modest St. John's Protestant Church, and Eleanor's schoolhouse.

Joshua did not pull back on Parbuckle's reins until he reached the jigsaw manors around Eleanor's eastern environs. After these Greek Revival and wood-trimmed Gothic brick residences came the courthouse and business blocks, where such establishments as the bank, library, Leroux's Assay Office, Katz's Drug Store, and the Occidental Hotel could be found. Most of these buildings were constructed of dressed bluish stone, peculiar to and carted over from the Lake City area.

The business day was drawing to a close as Joshua entered town. Word of Jon's death had made the rounds, and black-coated men leaving their offices respectfully tipped their stovepipe and beaver hats to Joshua. He would have ignored them, but Joshua knew Ella would have disapproved, so he nodded to each as he continued on west across the Tansey.

This half of Eleanor was populated with taverns such as the Telluride and Madam Wilding's Elysium, the sawmill, concentrators and smelters, *faux*-front stores like Baring-Gould's Mercantile and Crooke's Livery, the newspaper, a brewery, the jailhouse, and finally frame houses and log cabins. Joshua didn't stop, but kept going past the southern hills to St. Wenceslaus' churchyard, a God's acre of domesticated green grass, forlorn pines, and a couple of dozen graves enclosed by a brick wall.

Leaving the App to nibble grass beside the arched iron front gate, Joshua walked to the center of the cemetery. There, he stopped in front of a six-foot square tombstone hewn from the bluish Lake City stone. Chiseled prominently on all four of its sides was the name *LUTHER BRAND*.

"Hello, Father."

Joshua scanned the grounds to see if anyone was in earshot. When he was sure he was alone, "I'll assume if you can hear me that you know about Jon. Maybe he's with you, wherever you may be. I need to hash out an idea with you. I was looking at the Kirk's place a little bit ago, and it got me thinking that there may be a way to find Jon's killers. It's risky, and Ella and I will likely have a blowup when she finds out, but . . . Jon was my *son*. He was flesh of my flesh." His face grew as hard as the stone before him. "Whoever murdered my child *must* pay! *Must!* I know you would have risked everything if this had happened to you. I know you would. I only wish I could hear you tell me so yourself."

No answer.

Instead of continuing, he glanced across the path to the churchyard's next largest plot. A sandstone marker not half the size of Luther's stone was servicing three graves: Amos Kirk (hanged July 4, 1865), wife Lora (died January 6, 1847), and son Paul (December 31, 1862).

Joshua glanced back at his family's stone. More specifically, at a bullet gouge above the *U* in *LUTHER* on the north mare, the side facing the Kirks' plot. *"Risky" is right. I'm lucky to be alive.* A shiver jogged Joshua's body, almost hard enough to make him reconsider what he was going to do. *No! I have to do something. Anything! For Jon.*

Riding back across the Argos bridge to east Eleanor, Joshua went inside the Nox Building, his syndicate's headquarters. He climbed the stairs to the second floor where a telegrapher was on duty, day and night, seven days a week. Ondrej Hasek, a bright young man Joshua had hired away from the Denver and Rio Grande in March, was manning the post tonight.

"Mr. Brand?" Hasek rose, putting down his book, Peter Whitehorne's 1560 translation of Machiavelli's *The Art of War*. Joshua admired Hasek for always reading, always learning. "Sir, I heard about your son. I'm very . . ."

"I need to send a message to Chicago." Joshua spoke louder than necessary to cut off the young man. Grabbing paper and pen from Hasek's desk, he jotted the message and who it was meant for. "You send this in care of Pinkerton's."

"The detective agency?" The young man sounded intimidated.

"Now, Ondrej. And listen to me. Tell no one about this except the other telegraphers. Otherwise you send it and you forget about it or you'll find yourself back working for the D&RG tomorrow morning, this time as a baggage clerk." Joshua did not like making threats, but when he did, he was famous for keeping them.

"Of course, Mr. Brand." Hasek began translating the message into Morse code.

"You tell the other telegraphers that my caveat applies to them as well. If word of this gets out, I'll have the culprit's head. As for any reply, if or when there is one, you contact me immediately. Day or night. No matter the hour."

Joshua left without another word.

CHAPTER THREE

Three weeks later Ella Brand rambled through the Brands' Victorian at four in the morning.

Something had awoken her from a dreamless sleep. What it was she could not say. An urge, an inkling—she did not know and never would. She had to get out of bed and roam, searching for something but having no idea what.

Ella had not lit a candle, afraid she would wake her husband. No need. Her eyes, ample and the color of limes, were adjusted to the darkness.

Tiptoeing down the second floor corridor like a nocturnal dryad, her willowy body slipped in and out of the silvery light of the moon.

Ella was tall for a woman, nearly the same height as her husband, with small hips, small breasts, but legs lengthy enough to turn a champion trotter green. Life in the Rockies could be corrosive on a woman's good looks, but Eleanor Brand, at age thirty-two, appeared immune to the

harsh environment, as fresh and beautiful as a
schoolgirl. Her curly Irish raven hair, which
draped down her back when worn loose like it was
now, framed an angular face with high cheeks, an
aquiline nose, and perky lips. Everything about
Ella was either demure or sleek, except her thighs.
A passionate equestrian since age 3, Ella had the
quadriceps of a ballet dancer. These thighs
abashed Ella. She refused to indulge even in a pub-
lic bath while visiting New York or other old
states' metropolises because of them.

The woman wandered like a phantasm, downstairs and upstairs then downstairs again. Her
home was so still. Too still. She had never noticed
how hushed her home was during the watches of
the night. The silence threatened to smother her.
She ached to hear familiar noises like Juanita put-
tering in the kitchen or cleaning the parlor, or
Joshua working in the study, or Jon . . . well, Ella
had grown accustomed to Jon's absence over the
past year, but this was terribly different. Then Jon
had been away. Now he was dead, gone forever.

Only during the past couple of days could Ella
think about Jon without falling apart. *Poor Joshua,*
she mused. He had had to be strong for both of
them since the funeral. *Not that he complained.* No,
her husband would never permit himself to com-
plain, but even at her darkest she could not help
but notice how the man she loved had begun to
slow down to listen for his boy whenever he happened by Jon's bedroom door. Sometimes Joshua
dared to reach for the knob, to open the door and
peak inside, before moving on. She had seen him
on Parbuckle, these days riding at barely a canter,

never the proud pace he used to maintain, especially whenever Jon had ridden beside him. If Joshua picked up the pace at all nowadays it was only because he was in a hurry, and then her husband galloped as if trying to escape from something ineffable. Perhaps the same inexplicable urge or inkling that had compelled Ella from bed before dawn to haunt her own home.

What was that?

There! Out of the corner of her eye!

Candle light next door!

Ella back-tracked to the study to look out the windows at the house she grew up in. She searched but the light was gone. *But I could have sworn* . . . she had seen the flicker of candle light splitting the knotted planks nailed over the window to the nursery, which Amos had later converted into "The playroom."

Ella started to step into the study then shrieked when Joshua asked, "What about the playroom?" He was behind her. "I woke up and you were gone. I was scared."

She caught her breath and waited for her heart to shrink to its normal size again. "I didn't mean to worry you. But, honestly, I saw a light in the old playroom next door."

"You did?" Joshua did not sound like he doubted his wife as he walked past her into the study to stare out the window. For two full minutes he stood as still as a field mouse waiting out a circling hawk. "I don't see anything, dear."

"Neither do I . . . now."

Joshua went on facing the Kirk place. "Stray moonlight reflecting off the glass between those planks probably. They're getting old. Loose too. Might be time to replace them."

"Why bother? Raze the blasted place."

"Next year. This year's been hectic enough. If we're lucky a blizzard will come along this winter and bowl it over. Save us the expense and trouble."

"What trouble? A can of kerosene and a match will do the trick, Joshua."

She expected him to scold her. He always did when she let her tongue get ahead of her common sense. Not this time. He did not say anything for quite a few moments. Not until he seemed as sure as he could be that there was no sign of life next door. Only then did he turn around to hold her. "If it wasn't moonlight, maybe it was a nightmare."

"No. I haven't dreamed since . . ." She left off.

"Jon died." He filled in the blank. "So what's wrong?"

"I don't know. I awoke and had to . . . had to . . ."

"What?"

"I *can't* describe it. I just had to be up and about. That's it. That's all I know. I swear."

Unsure what to suggest, Joshua settled for, "Okay. Let's go back to bed."

"Not yet. I'm not ready yet. Please?"

"Okay."

They stayed in the corridor, holding each other, for several minutes. When they did go back to bed, neither slept for a long time.

Next door, a tall man departed the old Kirk house.

Standing in the shadow of the veranda, he slapped planks pried earlier off the front door back into place, careful to slip their nails into their original holes around the door frame. Leaving the porch, he glanced over his shoulder at the window to the playroom, then walked down the bluff towards town.

CHAPTER FOUR

The tall man entered the sheriff's office as a chanticleer crowed in the morning. Sitting alone behind one of two desks in the cracker-box front office, eating breakfast, was a man about twenty-five. He was handsome with coal forelocks falling over moon green eyes.

"Help you, mister?" Coleman asked between chews.

The deputy assayed that the stranger was a manhunter fresh off the trail. Rangy but tough, the stranger appeared to be in his middle to late thirties, stood about six-feet-two, and weighed roughly a hundred-eighty pounds. The stranger's light red hair was flecked with gray, his blue eyes pale enough to pass for silver, and his face tanned and scored from years of exposure to sun and wind. It was a good-looking face, rugged in the way women called "character," but also scary, like a bird of prey's. The stranger had a broad forehead, cheeks that tapered to a small chin, thin lips that were not accustomed to smiling, and a hawksbill nose. Strapped around the man's waist was an Army Colt .44-.40 in a Threeperson holster, and one sinewy hand hefted a Navy Arms Henry rifle of the same caliber.

"Sheriff in?" The man's voice was softer and more educated than Coleman had expected.

"Around six. Can I help you?" The deputy introduced himself.

"My name's Paul Kirk." The man reached into his coat pocket and pulled out a folded piece of paper. He handed it to Coleman. "I'd like that back, but you can show it to the sheriff when he comes in."

It was a telegram: $5000 IF YOU FIND SON'S KILLERS. The sender was JOSHUA BRAND. In the address in the telegram's upper left corner Coleman read: PINKERTON'S.

"You really from Pinkerton's, Mr. Kirk?"

"I work for them sometimes."

"Well, if Sheriff Moses knows about this, he didn't say anything to me. Sorry."

"Is *Jeb* Moses the sheriff? The old outlaw?"

"Uh-huh."

"Okay." There was respect in Kirk's tone. "Could you tell him I'm checking in with him as a courtesy? I'm heading over to the Occidental to take a bath and have some breakfast. I'll come back later this morning."

"I'm sure the sheriff will want to talk with you as soon as he gets in."

"Fine. I'd like to meet him. Of course he might

want to talk to Joshua Brand first. That's okay with me. It's been a long ride." Kirk moved for the door.

"Mr. Kirk, you might try the Canyon House first. It's a lot closer, just down the street, and a lot less expensive than the Occidental." He refrained from adding, "And the swankiest hotel between Denver and Leadville doesn't cater to saddle tramps."

"Thanks, but don't worry about me. I imagine that five thousand dollars will cover my bill." Kirk left.

Confident cuss, Coleman thought before reading the telegram a second time. "Boy, Mose isn't going to like this. Not one bit."

Kirk was sitting in a tub of hot water a half hour later, knees around his ears, juggling a brush with a bar of lye, when Moses opened the door to his hotel room without knocking.

"Would you close that door behind you?" the bather asked as he scrubbed his feet. "Even in mid-July morning drafts are chilly when you're soaking your bones."

Moses slammed it shut.

"Grateful to you."

"You know who I am?"

"I hope you're the sheriff," Kirk said, although he really had no doubts. Moses appeared to be all Kirk had heard, especially the sheriff's resemblance to a grizzly, right down to the bear's dark, cruel brown eyes. About the only inconsistency was Moses' mustache and hair, which were thick, not wiry, and shock white, not the copper color of a grizzly's coat.

Moses yanked Joshua's crumpled telegram from his shirt pocket. "You give this to my deputy?"

"Yes, sir. Thanks for returning it. Lay it by my rig, would you please?" The room was decorated with patterned wallpaper from Kansas City and furnished with a double-feather bed with a sleigh footboard, a dresser, a washstand, a secretary with chair for writing, and a round table with chairs for eating or card playing. Lying across the top of this table was Kirk's gunbelt and rifle.

"I'll just hold onto this. And I'd appreciate it if you came along with me. We're gonna have a chat with Mr. Brand."

"You can go on without me, sheriff. Let me know what Josh tells you."

Moses glowered at Kirk.

"Sheriff, I haven't had breakfast yet." Kirk climbed out of the tub and used a towel to dry off.

"I'm sure if Mr. Brand's willing to offer you five thousand bucks, he'll oblige you with some grub."

Kirk's laugh was a sad one. "Josh wouldn't spit in my mouth if I was dying of thirst."

"You talk like you two know each other." Moses walked to the round table, keeping one eye on Kirk while examining the firearms with the other.

"Of course we know each other." Finished with the towel, Kirk grabbed a pair of clean longjohns and trousers off the bed and started to get dressed. "I suppose he's never mentioned me."

"No, but I know your reputation, Mr. Kirk. You're a crackerjack bounty hunter. Wasn't aware you were a Pinkerton, though. So how do you know Mr. Brand?" Without asking permission, Moses grabbed the Henry for closer inspection. "Nice rig you've got here."

If Kirk minded, he did not let Moses see it. "Thanks. I'm afraid it's Pinkerton's policy never to discuss a client with anyone, not even the redoubtable Jeb Moses."

"What's that supposed to mean?" Moses put down the Henry and picked up the gunbelt.

Kirk slipped on his socks and boots, then moved to the washstand to use its mirror as he combed his hair. He was already shaved. "Formidable. Commanding respect."

Moses grunted, then chose to press on. "You already claim to know Josh Brand and his telegram says why you're here. So what's the big secret?"

"That's Pinkerton policy, Sheriff. It's nothing personal."

"I'm powerful glad to hear it, Mr. Kirk." Moses laid the gunbelt back on the table while Kirk opened a drawer in the dresser and pulled out a gingham shirt. "I've got a policy too. When my boss hires somebody else to do my job, I want to know why. Nothing personal."

Kirk was taken aback. "You work for Josh? Not the town?"

"Josh Brand *is* the town, Mr. Kirk. Maybe you don't know him as well as you pretend to."

"We haven't spoken for a few years." He tucked his shirt in his pants then stared at Moses. The large man stood between him and the round table. "I don't suppose you'd hand me my gunbelt?"

"No need for shooting irons, Mr. Kirk. Eleanor's

a peaceful place, and you'll be in my company."
The sheriff patted his holster. He grinned, too, but
it was not friendly.

Kirk grinned back. "Certainly."

Moses normally would not call on Joshua at home
before nine, but today, considering the circumstances, he was willing to make an exception.

Juanita answered the front door. The Brands
were still in bed, she said. Moses, again out of
character, insisted Mr. Brand would want to see
him. "Tell him Paul Kirk is with me. We'll wait in
the study."

"Actually," Kirk announced, "I'll wait out here."

"You can come with me." Moses reached for
Kirk, but Kirk stepped back and Moses missed.
"Sheriff, is this worth going to the grass over? Because the only way you're getting me inside is if
you drag me, which would be a monumental mistake. Trust me, Josh does not want me in his
home."

"Why's that?"

All Kirk would say is, "Pinkerton policy."

Moses did not like it, but told Juanita they
would wait on the porch for Mr. Brand.

The housemaid closed the door. Joshua opened
it again two minutes later wearing a paisley dress-
ing robe. Kirk's first impression was Brand
seemed tired but that the years had been kind to
him. Joshua, without looking at Kirk, asked
Moses, "What's he doing here?"

"You sent for him."

"I don't recall asking to talk to him."

"And I don't recall you telling me you signed on a manhunter!"

Joshua glared at Moses before closing the front door. "Keep your voice down. Ella's had a rough night. I don't want you waking her."

"I'm sorry to hear that, but, blast it! Why didn't you tell me about this? You're paying me to find these killers."

"Is that why you're here?" Joshua sounded low on patience. "Jeb, you and every lawman and scout for two hundred miles have had three years to run down these bushwhackers. *Three years!* Forgive me for thinking expert help is long overdue."

"Don't peddle me horse dung for loam! Three years didn't mean squat to you before Jon was killed!"

Joshua walked to the porch railing. Faced the town. "I want my son's killers apprehended and punished. That's the sole reason this man is here. You can help him, Jeb, or you can stay out of his way. That decision is entirely up to you." He went back inside without looking at Moses and Kirk.

Moses' chest heaved as if he had just run up the bluff. Kirk, unarmed and feeling vulnerable, was grateful when Moses finally stomped off the porch and said, "Follow me. I'll pay for your breakfast."

Ella Brand watched from behind the camouflage of the bedroom window's laced curtains as Moses and the manhunter left the porch. She was still there when her husband walked into the room, and he paled as she glanced at him then back out the window. "We must talk, Joshua."

* * *

"I warned you."

Moses screwed his eyes into Kirk's.

"I'm not trying to rub salt in a wound, Sheriff. You're riled and I don't blame you. I would be, too, if I were you."

"That supposed to cheer me up?"

A pretty waitress—Moses thought the cornsilk filly's name was Hope—brought Kirk a plate of eggs and bacon as the men sat at a table in the bar-room in the Telluride. This early in the morning, they had the place to themselves. Moses had suggested the Galena Cafe over on the west end, where the food was better and there would be people to brighten the day. Kirk had insisted on eating at the Telluride, though he would not explain why, a habit that was swiftly chafing Moses' patience.

Hope brought Kirk's coffee in a glazed porcelain mug, and he took a sip before digging into his plate. "I don't care if it does or doesn't. I'm just being honest. You don't want me here. Fine. I really don't want to be here."

"Well, here we are."

"It's hard to turn down five thousand dollars. Besides, the Brands and I have a history."

" 'The Brands'? Not 'Josh,' but both Brands?"

Kirk painted on a poker face as he swallowed a forkful of bacon slathered in runny yoke. *Pinkerton policy*, echoed in Moses' mind.

"Hang it, Kirk, if there's something I ought to know about you and the Brands, why don't you stop dancing around and tell me?"

Kirk did not get a chance to reply.

"*Paul* Kirk?"

A burly Irishman, about fifty, standing halfway between five and six feet tall and dressed in the scuffed wool pants, shirt, and vest of a miner, had planted himself behind Kirk's seat. The skin beneath the man's gray beard was cherry red, his black eyes barely visible under their lids.

Moses asked, "Something eating at you, Mike?"

"Mike?" Kirk had not reacted to the voice, but responded to the name. "Mike *Grell?*" He turned and beamed at the Irishman. "You're still here?"

"Aye. Still working for the Nox. No thanks to your old man."

Old man? Moses had no idea what Grell was talking about, so opened his ears and sat back.

"Sit down, Mike. Don't tell me you're still mining."

"I'm the foreman at the Erebus. This is my day off, and I thought I'd enjoy a dram a wee early, but I wouldn't have come in here if I knew the Telluride was serving your like. The next thing you know, they'll be allowing Chinamen in here."

Talk like that led to fights. Moses dropped his hand to his holster, prepared to discourage any violence before it began.

"What's wrong, Mike?" Kirk asked. "I haven't seen you since '62, and I don't recall parting on sour terms."

"That was before your old man tried selling the Nox and putting the whole bloody territory out of work, all for his own selfish spite."

"Look, Mike, I . . ."

"And what are you doing here, anyway? You're dead, last I heard. And better off you were, at least as far as folks like me are concerned. Killed defending the Union, wasn't it? There's a pretty grave for you, right beside your mother and no-account father in St. Wenceslaus' hallowed church-yard. So what happened, Paulie? Did you bolt when the guns got too loud? Found it easier to be thought as one of the honored dead rather than a deserting coward?"

"Mike Grell!" shouted Moses. "That's enough! Get over to the bar and shut your bazoo, or you're going to be spending your day off in the hoosegow. You listening, man?"

"I'll speak my peace. There's no law against that."

"Peace, my eye. This fellow's been nothing but sociable to you. Now draw rein."

"Seeing as you two are sitting here like friends, I'd expect you to defend him. You're a good man, Jeb, but as God is my witness Paul Kirk is the son of a harpy—"

Kirk had heard enough. He snatched his coffee cup with his left hand and whipped it across the miner's scalp. The cup shattered, coffee burned Kirk's wrist and Grell's neck, and the miner's legs collapsed. Pieces of porcelain were scattering before Moses could draw his gun. The sheriff had never seen anyone move as quick as Kirk, who glanced at Moses' gun and cocked his head. "What's that for?"

Moses was sweating. He had the drop on this human rattler, but was not sure what to do next.

"You said it yourself, Sheriff. I was nothing but polite to Mike. I let slide what he said about my fa-ther, but what kind of man would I be if I let him call my mother a 'harpy'?"

Hope ran into the bar, saw the prostrate Grell, and screamed.

Her scream snapped Moses out of his shock. Kirk was right. To a point, anyway. He put his revolver back in its holster and told the waitress, "Fetch Doc Gluzunov. Don't dally."

Hope did as told, careful to keep her distance from the men. Meanwhile a crowd from outside, alerted by the commotion and her scream, began drifting inside the Telluride to see what was happening.

Kirk asked, "You arresting me?"

Moses walked to the miner, squatted, and checked Grell's pulse. A little weak, but that was not unexpected.

"I didn't kill him."

"You want to tell me what he was busting a blister about?" Moses stood and made himself stare at Kirk's eyes. The manhunter was placid again. So were bobcats, from time to time, but that did not mean Moses ever wanted to be nose to snout with one.

Kirk, ashamed, tried but could not look at Grell. "My father's Amos Kirk."

"You're *that* Paul Kirk?" Even during Grell's tirade a connection between Eleanor's Kirks and the manhunter had never dawned on Moses.

"Yes, sir."

"You're Joshua Brand's brother-in-law? The *dead* one?"

The crowd inside the bar gawked at Kirk with abrupt recognition and disbelief.

"Not so dead." Kirk's voice was a whisper.

"Why didn't you tell me? Why didn't Joshua tell me any of this?"

"Must we talk here?" Kirk stared at the crowd.

Moses followed Kirk's gaze. "No. We can go to my office after the doc gets here."

"I appreciate it."

Kirk went on staring at the crowd a few moments more, then, suddenly, on second thought, turned towards Moses. Speaking so the crowd was sure to hear, "You wanted to know why I'm here. Because Ella Brand's my sister, and Jon Brand was her son. I'm here to find Jon's killers. This is about family." Facing the crowd again, he finished with, "All of it is about family."

CHAPTER FIVE

Eddie Foy took a seat at the faro table. Not to play, but to pay his respects to the dealer.

"I am sorry to hear you're leaving Dodge, Miss Penny."

Penelope Fairchild—blond, twenty-three, pretty but resolute in build and will, without a hint of innocence—had been sitting alone. She had come to The Variety saloon for an early breakfast and, not in the mood to return home, had decided to pass some time at her table playing Patience.

"Thank you, Mr. Foy." Soft-spoken with a Yankee lilt, Penny's voice was nonetheless firm, even though she seemed surprised to see him. "I thought you had enlisted in one of the detachments. Aren't you going to Colorado too?"

"What put such an idea into your head?"

"Doc Holliday said he invited you."

The sprightly little Midwesterner laughed. "That's true, he did, but I'm no fighter." Foy was a

popular comedian in a variety troop appearing at
the Comique Theatre. He leaned forward to whisper, "Besides, I've only been in Dodge since the
first of June. Why would I risk my life in what is
arguably a local matter?"

"I wish my papa saw things your way." Penny
and her parents, Bartholomew and Kathryn, had
not been in Kansas much longer than Foy's troop.
Residents of Dallas for the past four years, the
Fairchilds had abandoned Texas only to discover
that Dodge City's glory days as the latest capital
of a reinvigorated terminus circuit were fading
with the spring thaw. Undeterred, merchants
Bartholomew and Kathryn set up shop while
Penny, cool-headed and sharp with cards, found a
job south of the railroad tracks at Ham Bell's Variety dealing faro and poker. Life for the Fairchilds
settled back into as normal a routine as family life
can get in a terminus town, until railroad agent
J.H. Phillips of the Atchison, Topeka, and Santa Fe
thundered in a few days earlier. Service to
Leadville, the West's newest wonder city, was in
contest and the D&RG had organized a militia to
drive the Santa Fe out of Colorado. Phillips was
hiring gunmen, and Bartholomew jumped at the
chance to fight for the Kansas-chartered railroad
line, so long as he did not have to leave his family
in Dodge City. Assigned to Captain John Joshua
Webb, Bartholomew was permitted time to pack
up so the Fairchilds could accompany Ben Thompson's detachment of janissaries to Cañon City.

"Miss Penny," Foy opined, "I'm afraid some
men are born with more than their share of red
pepper. That doesn't mean your father will be

foolhardy. As far as I know, no one's even been shot or hung over this issue. Merely roughed up a bit and shown the way out of town."

Penny collected her cards and shuffled. Her father's decision had nothing to do with high spirits, but rather than tell Foy this, she asked, "What can you tell me about Colorado?" Foy had spent the past winter in Leadville.

"Denver appears headed for great things, and Leadville is as civilized as any town that prospered during the gold fever days. Once this railroad issue is settled I suspect your family could do well for yourselves there. They will be mining silver out of the San Juans for years to come. In the long run this will probably turn out to be a wonderful opportunity for the Fairchilds."

"I hear Colorado is cold in the winter." She cut the deck with her right hand.

"That it is. This time of year, though, the mountains are a paradise. A veritable paradise."

Penny filliped a card on the table. The queen of diamonds. *At least it's not the queen of spades*, she thought. "I hope you're right about this being an opportunity for my family, Mr. Foy. I sincerely hope you are."

Ella and Joshua Brand strolled up Argos Avenue to the jailhouse to find Moses standing on the sidewalk watching day turn to dusk. The sheriff wondered if the couple had had a spat. He couldn't recall ever seeing them walking together when Ella didn't have her hand on Joshua's arm.

"Good afternoon, Jeb," she said. "Can you spare a moment for some friends?"

"Sure enough. Got coffee brewing for my supper if you'd like some."

Joshua passed but his wife accepted as he followed her and Moses inside.

Moses pulled up a chair for Ella and brushed off its seat. She sat as he poured a cup, then repeated the favor for himself.

"If you're worried about your brother, Ella, don't be. I ain't going to arrest him."

"So I heard. Are you sure that's a wise decision?"

Moses' left eye twitched. "Why?"

"He attacked one of our men."

"Maybe you didn't hear, but your brother was defending your mother."

"That's beside the point."

Surprise blotted the sheriff's face.

"My name is Mrs. Joshua Brand," she continued. "I have no ties to or sympathies for the Kirks."

"Ella, that don't sound like you. You love your family." Moses glanced at Joshua, who was standing behind his wife, as motionless as a statue.

"Jeb, I realize this happened before you became sheriff, but you must know that Amos Kirk was hanged for murdering Luther Brand."

"Well, sure I do. That's about all I know though."

"I see. Then I should tell you that Amos never approved of Joshua and I getting married. That's why we eloped a few days before Joshua left to volunteer for the war with Paul. Soon after Joshua returned home, Amos attempted to sell the Kirks' share of the Nox to a Spanish syndicate so Amos could drag Jon and me away from Eleanor. If that sale had gone through, the new syndicate would have fired everyone working for Nox and replaced them with their own men. That would have put most of the people living in Eleanor out of work. When Luther found out, he tried to stop Amos. That's when Amos killed him."

"Oh." It was all Moses could think of to say, except, "But, Ella, your *mother*?"

"I never knew her. She died giving birth to me."

"I see." Moses thought that would have made Ella feel more protective of the woman, not less, but kept that opinion to himself. "All right, then. Your name's Brand, not Kirk. Fine. Why do you think I should have arrested your brother? Josh, you hired him to find Jon's killers. He sure can't do that locked up in the calaboose."

Before Joshua could answer, Ella interjected with, "Finding Jon's killer is your job."

Moses glared at Joshua as he told Ella, "I would think you'd know better than me that Josh ain't happy with the way I'm doing my job."

"That's not true, Jeb," Joshua protested, coming to life. "I never intended you to get that impression."

" 'Three years,' you said. That, and 'Forgive me for thinking expert help is long overdue.' Oh, and let's not forget the part about you wanting Jon's killers punished, and that was the sole reason Kirk was here. Now you want to tell me how I could've gotten the wrong impression?"

Ella craned her neck and looked at her husband as if reconsidering something about him as Joshua asked Moses, "Do you deny that Paul Kirk is an expert manhunter?"

Moses squinted. "Don't talk at me like a Denver lawyer, Josh! You know that ain't what I meant!"

"Look, Jeb, I know Paul. He was my best friend when we grew up, and when Ella and I eloped he was my best man. We went to war together. Fought side by side."

"Fine. You know Paul Kirk. He's an upstanding man. Why does that make you think he can find the bushwhackers when folks who know this territory better than anyone haven't dug up squat?"

"Paul's character has nothing to do with his abilities. You only know him by reputation. I know that Paul Kirk's reputation doesn't do him justice. If he can't track the men who killed Jon, he'll outsmart them. He's always been that way, just like his father. Both could be scary clever when it came to figuring out people."

Ella's eyes suddenly blazed as she shot Joshua a look that made her husband wither. "I believe Moses is talking sense. Especially since there is no way you can be sure my brother is still the man you remember." She faced Moses. "I understand that Joshua is impatient. He loves Jon so. And, for the past few weeks, Joshua's had to be the strong one in our family. It's time for me to start pulling my share of the load."

"Meaning?" Joshua asked the back of her head.

"I grew up with Paul too. I knew Paul Kirk all of my life until I was fifteen, and I'm afraid he could have become as dangerous and deceitful a man as our father turned out to be. If I'm wrong about that, then God forgive me. Nevertheless, Paul should be in jail for hurting Mr. Grell." Ella placed her cup on Moses' desk and stood. "That's my piece, and I've said it. I appreciate you listening, Jeb."

"Sure thing. I'm sorry if I lost my temper."

"No. I understand. Trust me. Good evening."

Ella led her husband outside. Moses picked her cup up and followed them out to dump her coffee into the street. As the Brands walked away from the jailhouse, the sheriff glimpsed Paul Kirk standing in the road by the sidewalk waiting for the couple.

"Ella?"

The Brands started to walk past Paul.

"Ella!"

The shout flustered Mrs. Brand, who turned and asked her brother to please lower his voice. "What will people think?"

"Who cares? I only want to talk to you."

The Brands walked towards Paul. Ella said, "If there's something you need to discuss with me, come to the house sometime."

"I'm not welcomed there." Paul shot Joshua a glance. "Besides, all I wanted was to tell you I never meant to get in a fuss with Mike. He left me no choice. I hope you understand."

"I have already discussed my feelings on the subject with Sheriff Moses."

"Okay." Paul didn't appear sure what to think about that, an appearance he didn't seem accustomed to assuming. "It is nice to see you again, sis. And I am so very sorry about Jon. More than I can say."

Her brother's concern seemed to soften Ella. "Thank you, Paul."

Moses was sure he saw a hint of kindness flash

in Ella's eyes, and Paul warm up to that flash like a winter rose in a chinook breeze. It also appeared that Ella was getting ready to say something more until Joshua cut in. "We do have business, Ella." And with that, Joshua led his wife down Argos again. Paul seemed to wilt as the couple walked off. The manhunter waited for a parting glance from Ella, and when it didn't come, he moved to the sidewalk and walked away.

Coleman came up the other end of Argos. "Hey, Mose."

"Teddy." The men went inside the jailhouse.

"Was that the Brands I saw talking to Mr. Kirk?"

"If you can call that talking."

"Is it true what I've been hearing? That this Paul Kirk is Mrs. Brand's brother?"

"It's true." Moses set Ella's cup near the stove.

"Well, I'll be! So he didn't die at Murfreesboro like Mr. Brand thought."

"I guess not." Moses almost let what Coleman said slip by him. "It was Josh who claimed Kirk died in the war?"

"Well, the War Department couldn't find a body, so Mr. Brand had to testify one way or the other since he was the last one to see Kirk alive, so to speak. My maw had a cousin who had to do the same thing for a friend after Bull Run."

"Uh-huh." That sounded logical to Moses. At least he thought it did.

"So what brought the Brands to our side of the Tansey? I can't recall them visiting the jail before."

Moses sat silent as he recollected the scene at the Telluride that morning. Ella had not been exaggerating when she'd called her brother a dangerous man.

"Teddy, how much do you know about the Kirks and the Brands? Besides scuttlebutt and gospel mill gossip?"

"Oh, not much more than you, I reckon. Only thing that comes to mind is that old saw about Luther Brand being the head of the town's vigilante committee. I never believed it."

Moses didn't bother to tell his deputy that Luther Brand had not only been the committee's big bug, the man had actually founded it, though Luther's brand of vigilantism tended to be less concerned with outlaws and more about runaway slaves, suspicious Mexicans, and renegade Indians. "Anything else?"

"No. Why?"

There was something more Ella had said that kept tickling Moses' funny bone of caution: *I knew Paul Kirk all of my life until I was fifteen*. Following a hunch, Moses told Coleman to mind the store while he paid a call on the telegraph office.

CHAPTER SIX

Kirk dotted his last "i" then rubbed both of his own: "What time is it, please?"

Ned Scott, editor of the *Eleanor Epitaph*, looked up from cleaning his Washington hand press. "Seven-past-eleven."

Eight hours, Kirk thought. Except for taking a break to talk with Ella after he noticed his sister and Joshua head for the jailhouse, he had been reading and scribbling notes for a third of a day. *No wonder I feel like I tramped through a sandstorm.* "I apologize if I've kept you, Mr. Scott."

"My name's Ned, and long hours are nothing unusual for me. Anyway, it's satisfying to see somebody pouring over my work the way you have. I hope it hasn't been fruitless, Mr. Kirk."

"Paul." It was nice to talk to a friendly person again after that morning. Scott had moved to Eleanor from Omaha in '67 with his shirt tail full of type, so he had not been affected by Amos' crimes. "My compliments to the observations in your reporting. You'd make a good Pinkerton."

Wiping ink from his hands, Scott chuckled. "Last I heard Allan Pinkerton disapproves of hiring cowards." He pulled a bottle of Hottom's from his desk drawer. "Care for a drop? There's whiskey in the typesetter's desk, next to my revolver, if you prefer that."

"Sherry's fine, thank you. Why did you call yourself a coward? I've never met a frontier journalist who didn't have more backbone than good sense."

"You give me too much credit, but I'll accept it." Scott clinked glasses with Kirk. "Best of luck to you," he toasted, then sipped.

"How to," Kirk offered back.

"So, did you find anything useful about the cross killers? I'm eager to write the end of this story."

Kirk stared at the piles of *Epitaphs* dating back a few weeks prior to the first bushwhacking on August 14, 1876. "Hopefully a start. I plan to ride over to Lake City and compare and contrast my notes with Harry Woods at the *Silver World*. I'd also like to see where the killings occurred for myself."

"I'll eat my hat if Woods knows anything I don't. Eleanor has been in the hub of these cross killings, and I've talked at great length to every authority who's been involved. Sheriffs, coroners, the U.S. marshal, scouts, even Dave Cook's hands-up detectives. Everything there is to know is in my articles."

"I can't chance that you've overlooked something. As it is, your articles fail to infer conclusions from what you have learned."

Scott gave Kirk a look. "Really? Care to give me a for-instance?"

"If you like. These bushwhackers are superb shots."

"Well, that goes without saying."

"I said, 'superb.' I doubt there are even ten Kentuckians who could shoot twenty-seven people in the head from an average distance of over two hundred yards without a miss."

"Hold up now. How can you suggest they've never missed? And some folks may assume there are more than one killer, but no one knows for certain if this is the work of one man or many."

"There are three killers. Well, at least three."

"How do you come by that particular number?"

"Think about it. Most of these bushwhackings were committed on a single individual, but six were committed on walking parties of two or three people. According to your articles, none of the victims were moved by the bushwhackers, except to roll a body over to expose the chest. Now, in these six attacks, the victims were always found in close proximity to one another. No further apart than members of a walking party might be expected to keep together while traveling for their own protection."

Scott had a glimmer of where Kirk was heading. "If the cross killers had missed, a victim would have had the chance to react to being fired upon. He would have run for cover."

"If he had, he would have been found laying away from his companion or companions. None were. Also, the descriptions of the victims' bodies and footprints indicate that they were all shot in their tracks and not in flight. How is that possible, unless the victims of all six of these attacks were shot simultaneously? Since three of the parties consisted of three victims, and the bushwhackers have never attacked groups of more than three, there must be at least three shooters."

Scott slapped his forehead. "Why didn't I realize that?"

"Don't fret about it. A newspaperman's job is to observe, not surmise." Kirk smiled.

"What else did I overlook?"

"Well, let me say first that, so far, I agree with you, Sheriff Moses, and Colonel Adams. These bushwhackings are not the work of Indians. At least not any tribe whose methods of ambush I am familiar with. I will consult with my own Indian authority about that, though, just to be safe."

"I suppose I should take some solace in that." Scott poured himself more sherry.

"These aren't cold-blooded murders, Ned. The motive for these crimes must be very personal to the bushwhackers."

"What makes you say that? Shooting someone from three hundred yards away? That's impersonal. The victims in the separate attacks have no association with each other, which suggests that they were selected at random. And a random killing is impersonal."

"All true." Kirk did not say it, but he would have bet that the bushwhackers had never even laid eyes on their victims until the killers were framing the poor devils in their sights. "On the other hand, mutilating *twenty-seven* people by carving an **X** into their breastbones? Over the course of three years? That's not only personal, it's obsessive."

"Maybe. Okay, let's say this *is* personal. Why exactly are they doing this?"

Kirk drummed his fingers on the table. "I think about that and I keep coming back to the crosses. Why an X? Illiterate men sign their names with an X. Could the bushwhackers be signing their work, like artists do? That makes sense if the motive behind the X is to make sure we know the bushwhackers are responsible for these particular killings. But why would that be so important that they risk the trouble involved with marking their victims? Why aren't their marksmanship and the lack of any trail signature enough? Considering their skills, the idea it's for the pure sadistic thrill of mutilation seems nonsensical. Apaches or Utes scalp their victims so they can display a trophy of their kills, but carving an X in a dead man's chest isn't the same thing as collecting a scalp. These bushwhackers haven't taken any kind of trophies, in fact, unless you count their victims' lives. Not one of the twenty-seven has been so much as robbed. These bushwhackers are behaving more like merchants taking an inventory. 'I killed this man. Cross him off, onto the next.'"

"All very interesting, I confess, but you haven't answered my question. Do you know why they are doing this?"

Kirk drummed and deliberated, then, after nearly a minute, "Can I have a little more sherry, Ned?"

The next morning Kirk stepped out of St. Wenceslaus with hat in hand. The day, less than an hour old, was already bright and humid.

Father Myers followed Kirk outside. "Feels like it's going to be a warm one." The priest, half a decade older than Kirk, had moved to Eleanor in 1865, succeeding St. Wenceslaus' first priest, Father Campbell. "That's July for you."

"August will be worse. Thanks for telling me what you could about Jon, Father."

"Glad to, Paul. I'm only sorry you never had the chance to meet him. True, Jon was between hay and grass, but you two strike me as being quite a bit alike."

"That's kind of you to say."

"I hope you will be able to work things out with Ella soon. There's so much more she and Joshua could tell you about their son."

"I'd like nothing better myself."

"Would you like to visit your parents before you go?"

That caught Kirk off guard, and he tried not to stammer as Myers led him into the churchyard.

"A man should never forget to honor his mother and father, Paul, nor be ashamed of them."

"No, Father, it isn't that." He glanced over at the bullet gouge above Luther's name in the Brand marker. "My name is on the stone is all."

"That shouldn't embarrass you. You're hardly the only veteran who was supposedly killed during the war. Maybe you'd like me to leave so you can pray alone?"

Kirk almost moaned. "Father, I'd be obliged if you could do the honors. Please. This isn't what I'm good at."

"Certainly, if you feel that way, Paul." They bowed heads. "Heavenly Father, the son of Amos and Lora Kirk has returned home. He asks that You watch over the souls of his parents, and the soul of his nephew, Jon Brand. And, Father, I ask that You watch over Paul. To guide him in this task he has undertaken and protect him from the dangers that lay ahead. Please bring him safely home again. Amen."

"Amen." Kirk shook Myers' hand, but could not quite look the priest in the face. "Thanks, Father. I owe you."

"You take care, Paul. Don't forget, there'll always be a place for you at St. Wenceslaus."

Kirk stayed behind as the priest walked back towards the church. "Father?"

"Yes?"

Kirk just noticed it. "Who tends to our grave? There aren't any weeds or wildflowers anywhere near our marker." He could not stop himself from hoping it was Ella.

"The church. Or, I should say, I do. Your father left a goodly amount to St. Wenceslaus."

"Oh. You do good work, Father."

"That's my aim."

Alone, Kirk looked at the names on the sandstone marker. "Amos." "Lora." His own. *If that isn't humbling*, he thought, *I don't know what is.* Humbling and inevitable.

"Got work to do." Putting on his hat, he left the churchyard.

Kirk glared toward the wagon trail from the top of the low knoll, at the spot where Coleman was indicating Jon Brand fell. Jon would have appeared small from here, as did the deputy, and doubtless helpless to whoever shot him. The assassin had selected an admirable killsite. Even if the first bullet had missed, there was nowhere for Jon to run for cover, and the chance of Jon seeing where it had come from and returning fire in time was nonexistent. All Jon could have done was flee, but it was doubtful the assassin would have missed twice.

"Varmints. No good varmints." Kirk did not bow his head, but he did repeat Father Myers' request that God watch over Jon's soul. "I swear I'll make right by you, Jon, or die trying."

He returned to the wagon trail and thanked Coleman.

"Welcome, Mr. Kirk. See anything I missed?"

"No, nothing like that. You heading back to town?" Kirk stepped up into his grulla's saddle.

"In a few minutes. I like it out here. Maybe I'll take my own look around. You never know. Still going to Lake City?"

"Uh-huh." Kirk cocked his head. "You know, from what I've read in the *Epitaph*, you and Sheriff Moses did everything you could to bring these bushwhackers to justice."

Coleman swallowed as he looked at the San Juans. "That don't do Jon much good."

"No. No, it doesn't. Did you know him?"

"Not really. I left school the year after Jon started. Besides, I belong to the wool hat bunch. I know he was a hard worker, like his paw, and those two loved each other. I can promise you that, Mr. Kirk. You just had to see them together to know they'd do anything for each other."

Apparently, Kirk thought. "I better be going to Lake City."

"Take it easy on your way. That's a hard ride."

"This pootin' pony and I are use to hard rides. You be careful." Horse and rider galloped off before the deputy could return the sentiment.

Coleman would have liked to join the man-hunter. He suspected he could learn a lot from Kirk, and, while some of Eleanor's citizens would disagree, he liked—"*What?*"

He snatched his revolver from its harness, and aimed it where Kirk had been standing at the top of the knoll. All before he realized what he was doing or what he was reacting to.

Staring down his sight, he saw . . . nothing.

But Coleman was positive he had seen someone up there out of the corner of one eye.

CHAPTER SEVEN

"An Indian?"

Moses stared at Coleman. He had been enjoying some coffee and a spirited debate about the AT&SF and D&RG when his deputy rushed into the Galena Café. Moses paid up then motioned Coleman to follow him outside.

"Didn't you hear me, Mose?"

"Everyone in the Galena heard you, Teddy."

"But, Mose—"

"Y'suppose we can discuss this at the jail?" he snapped.

Coleman walked two steps behind Moses all the way, as quiet as a boy about to get the switch. As soon as Moses closed the jailhouse door, "Hang it, Teddy! Sometimes I swear you ain't got the sense God gave a greener!"

The deputy did not know what to say.

"Did you forget what happened at the White River Agency last fall? Nathan Meeker and eleven employees dead, along with Major Thornburg and twelve cavalrymen sent to help them! And maybe you ain't heard, but the northern Utes have been kicking up the sundance again these past few weeks!"

"I have, but, Mose . . ."

"*But* you couldn't stop and think about that! You had to blather what you might have saw out on the tableland *in the Galena!* Half of Eleanor most likely knows what you said by now!"

"I thought you should know."

"Of course I should know! Ain't you listening to me? It's *where* you told me that's the problem!"

Coleman reddened. "I got carried away. I'm sorry."

"Uh-huh." Moses stopped to catch his breath. He despised losing his temper with his deputy. "What sort of Indian was he? Ute? Rapahoe? Cheyenne?"

"I can't say. He was wearing white man's clothes."

"You sure it was an Indian?"

"I'm sure." Coleman tried his best to sound positive.

"Uh-huh. Could you see if he was armed?"

"He had a large rifle, carried it proper, but he was too far away for me to be able to tell exactly what kind."

"Uh-huh. Anything else?"

Coleman could not think of more to add.

"Let me see. You're sure you saw an Indian, for maybe a second, dressed in white man's clothes and lugging a fair-sized rifle?"

"Yes."

"If this fellow was a cross killer, mind telling me why you ain't dead?"

"Well . . . uh . . ."

"Or why he couldn't have been a buffalo hunter or some other sort?"

"I don't, well, I didn't think of that."

"You *just didn't think*, boy." Moses suddenly felt old. "Ain't it bad enough I got Josh hiring a dead man to do my job and Ella telling me she wishes I'd arrested her own brother? Now you're running around like Chicken Little. I swear, Teddy, if the lot of you don't give me apoplexy, I must be immune to it."

When Ella had not asked for breakfast by ten o'clock, Juanita went ahead and carried a tray up to the Brands' bedroom. The mistress of the house was awake, but she did not so much as glance at the servant as Juanita set the tray on the nightstand.

"*Cómo usted se siente esta mañana, Señorita Ella?*"

"*Yo'm no muy hambriento, Juanita. Gracias.*"

"*Usted tiene que comer. Para mantenerse al ritmo de su fuerza. Permita que mí venga espalda para la bandeja en unos pocos minutos.*"

Ella was still upset at her husband for hiring her brother and in no mood to banter with Juanita, so the simplest thing to do seemed to be to feign acquiescence. "*Todo derecho.*"

Juanita left the tray while Ella tried to occupy her mind by tracing the intricate whirls and scrolls of the bedroom's millwork with her eyes. For the thousandth time, for all the good it did. What little sleep Ella did get the night before had been upset by an atrocious dream that still haunted her no matter how hard she tried not to think about it.

Ella had been walking down the hall towards Jon's room, inside which she heard a woman humming "Blue-Tail Fly" in a lullaby tempo. Another voice, sounding like Jon's when he was a boy, was calling for Ella. Not "Mamma," as Jon always did, but "Ella."

"I want to come home, Ella. Let me come home, Ella." Over and over, again and again.

Jon's door was closed. Ella reached for the knob but hesitated, like she had seen Joshua do, then opened the door.

A woman wearing slave clothes was rocking in the bedroom with her back turned towards Ella. Except this was not Jon's bedroom. It was the nursery in the Kirk house. Sitting at the woman's feet was Jon, maybe age twelve. He looked up and Ella saw that Jon's hair was not its normal black, but rather a strawberry blond. And when he spoke, she did not hear Jon's voice. It was Paul's.

"I want to come home, Ella. Let me come home, Ella."

How could Joshua have hired her brother without consulting her?

Because I would have forbidden it.

Not that Ella could fault Joshua's logic. After everyone else who tried had failed, including poor Jeb, her brother probably was their last hope of bringing Jon's killer—or killers—to task.

Except now Jon's reputation is at risk. How will he ever rest easy if our family is disgraced? And so long as

Paul is here that risk is terribly real. And what if vengeance is the reason Paul accepted Joshua's offer? What if he wants to ruin my family? Try as she might, Ella Brand could not stop working that worry over in her mind.

Until the smell of spice broke her concentration. Unable to remember the last time she had bothered to eat, Ella peeked at Juanita's tray and saw cinnamon toast, fresh milk, and a note from Joshua. She snatched the paper to tear it up before remembering she had never destroyed any of her husband's notes. Every one was stored in a trunk in the attic, tied in stacks by red ribbon. Her husband, reserved by nature, often communicated his feelings by writing personal missives, either on the spur of the moment, or after long thought while away from Ella, or even while in the same room with her. What precedent would she be setting, what fates put into motion, if she destroyed one now?

She decided to read his note before passing judgment on it:

To my heart,

I cannot apologize enough for the pain I have caused you by doing what I thought was right. What, I cannot deny, I still think was right. Nevertheless, you did not deserve to suffer any further heartache, and it is unforgivable that my actions caused you just that.

The dawn is rising after the first night we have spent apart under the same roof since we pledged our troth to each other. It has been ghastly not having you laying beside me on my left all night. I cannot describe the ache your absence still causes me. Do you know, dear Ella, that you curl your fist beneath your chin when you sleep? I know this because I have watched you do this over many, many dawns.

I hope some time—some day—you will allow me into your heart again. I am nothing without you, and am only myself when we are whole. If the day arrives that you feel you can forgive me, I beg that you tell me. That will be the first day of light I shall have known since we lost our beautiful boy.

*Your faithful,
Joshua*

Ella read the note again. As a tear rolled down one cheek, she folded the paper and laid it on her breast, not sure what to do next.

"God," she prayed, "why is this happening? Why?"

The Fairchilds, experienced pilgrims of the circuit, had their possessions and home packed and loaded for transport in plenty of time to board the AT&SF train taking the Kansas route out of Dodge City with Thompson's detachment.

"Can't say I'm sorry to bid farewell to that town," Bartholomew chuckled as the fading terminus capital rolled past his window.

Kathryn, respectful, nodded. "I will not miss the smell of buffalo hides, I must confess."

"Me, neither, Mother." Bartholomew patted her knee then smiled at his daughter. She sat across from them reading William Paley's *Evidences*. "How's your book, Sunflower?"

Penny commented it would serve to pass the time during their journey.

"That it should." He held up his own book, a collection of Robert G. Ingersoll's lectures. "It's only square to give both sides a show, but I think Bob Ingersoll lays all over Paley."

"I suppose, Papa."

Bartholomew almost asked his daughter if she were feeling well. She normally relished a good debate on any topic.

Kathryn commented that the conductor had told her the train would run parallel with the Arkansas River all the way to Pueblo and Cañon City. "We should arrive before supper. Can you imagine? The speeds these trains travel."

"They are a marvel," her husband agreed. "One more example of the magnificence of this frontier. Anything can happen here. The west is a wonderland. Where else can a bonanza be laid like an egg in your hat, even while you're sleeping soaked in someone's barn?"

Bartholomew paused to give his daughter a chance for rebuttal, but Penny, reading, did not feel obliged to join in the conversation.

He tried another tactic. "Mother's brought pemmican, in case you get hungry."

"Thank you, Mama." Her eyes never left her book.

Bartholomew turned to Kathryn for advice. His wife nudged with her elbow to say, "Talk to your daughter! This is your doing!"

"Sunflower, won't you tell us if anything's worrying you?" Outside their window, there was nothing but prairie, the Arkansas too far away to see.

"It's not my place, Papa."

Dutiful to a fault, he thought. "That's nonsense. You're a grown woman, Penelope. Stop hiding behind that book and talk to us."

She placed the *Evidences* in her lap. "I'm frightened, Papa."

"Because I'm fighting for the Santa Fe?"

"Because you're so anxious to fight. Anxious, I know, for the chance to prove you are as worthy of grace as Boston Corbett."

Bartholomew's face blanched as Kathryn cautiously reminded her husband, "You wanted her to speak her mind."

"I didn't give her leave to insult me!"

Penny, face placid but eyes as devoted as they were brown, told her father she loved him. "You're a brave man. You have nothing to prove."

Bartholomew was too honest to deny to his own blood that what she suspected did have a great deal to do with his signing on to help the Santa Fe. He also could not clam up after urging Penny to unpack her troubles.

"Would you believe me if I told you there is much more to my motive than what you think?" Bartholomew asked.

"I believe you do."

"Mr. Phillips is paying me more for a few days' work than we could ever earn in two years on our own. This is our bonanza! You'll be able to return east and finish your education, while Mama and I can quit the terminus circuit and settle down."

"Mr. Phillips hired the most esteemed of Dodge City's gunmen, and is spreading word throughout Colorado that men like Doc Holliday and Bat Masterson are working for the Santa Fe. It's a wise strategy considering the circumstances, but I cannot see why it must include you."

"Why? Can't I hold my own alongside Doc and Bat?"

"You can without doubt, Papa."

Penny had utter faith in her father's superior skills with artillery and dirk. He had proved them in June of 1864 when his detachment from the 16th New York Cavalry was cornered by Colonel John S. Mosby's raiders at Culpepper Courthouse. Ultimately, Bartholomew and one comrade, Boston Corbett, were the last Union soldiers alive, but the pair refused to quit fighting. Mosby was so impressed that he spared them, but demonstrated no pity by shipping Bartholomew and Corbett to Andersonville. While Bartholomew bucked the odds and survived almost a year in that, "Hell on earth where it takes seven of its occupants to make a shadow," Corbett came down with scurvy after three months and was transferred to Millen, Georgia. Corbett recovered, escaped, rejoined the 16th, was promoted to the rank of sergeant, and, on April 26, 1865, shot John Wilkes Booth dead at Garret's farm.

"I'm suggesting," Penny continued, "that you are alive because of your admirable courage in the face of withering adversity. I disapprove, however, of your working for the Santa Fe because I believe you have not a thing to prove, to God and least of all to yourself." Penny returned to Paley's *Evidences*.

Not sure what else to do, Kathryn started knitting.

Bartholomew, at a loss for what to say—much less think or feel—faced his window and watched Kansas roll past.

CHAPTER EIGHT

The sun was starting to set by the time Kirk reached Lake City, population 2,500.

Leading his horse down Silver Street, Kirk soon found the *Silver World*'s office. Harry Woods was there working late, but the newspaperman was more than happy to try and assist the manhunter. Two hours later Kirk left Woods' office and peeked up at a sneering sliver of moon high above Engineer Mountain. Kirk frowned; he had learned nothing new.

After renting a room for the night at the nearest hotel, Kirk liveried his grulla and then ventured past stores and churches on his way down to the town's Hell's Acre. "You'll find a saloon called The Amalgam down by Henson Creek, and it serves the best Texas beefsteak on the Western Slope," Woods had confided to Kirk. "The whiskey's okay, too, but the beer's better. The Amalgam can get rowdy after the miners show up after dark, but that shouldn't bother an hombre like you."

"I suppose not."

The Amalgam was a long, low log structure with a canvas roof. And it was doing a business. The dance floor was bustling with men and working girls as a violinist and trumpeter played *The Ocean Wave*. Meanwhile, a passel of sourdough miners—slathered from head to toe with dirt and rock dust except where whiskey had cleaned off their mustaches and beards—congregated around the bar. Kirk threaded his way through the miners, curious to overhear phrases like "rose-cheeked Adonis" and "honey-tongued" being bandied with vigor and some petulance as he made his way to the bar.

Waiting at the bar after ordering his steak, Kirk sipped on a beer, feeling more at home than he had since returning to the San Juans. Kirk liked miners. He had been raised around them and worked beside them. Amos Kirk and Luther Brand hadn't wanted their sons growing up without knowing firsthand about the strains, joys, benefits, and rewards that could only be experienced by hard labor. So, as soon as Paul and Joshua could lift a shovel and pick, the boys were sent into Nox' Erebus mine. Young Paul didn't like doing the work at first, but looking back now it was a lesson that Amos' son couldn't deny had made him a better man.

"What say you, friend?" someone asked Kirk, who turned toward the voice and saw a group of miners staring at him.

Kirk said, "Pardon me?"

The biggest of the miners, a hirsute man who appeared capable of ripping a stump out of the rockiest soil with his bare hands, wanted to know, "What say you? Is Shakespeare Bacon?"

Kirk cocked his head. Suddenly those curious phrases made sense, but to be sure he asked, "Are you talking about William Shakespeare and Francis Bacon?"

"Who else?" The big miner spoke with a southern accent. Probably Georgian, Kirk thought, since the man's deep drawl made it sound like he had rollers in his nose.

Next a spry, lean graybeard came scooting around from behind the hirsute man. "Ya look like a canny lad. Surely ya can't be *fyeul* enough ta believe Bacon could ha' wrote *Macbeth* or *A Midsummer's Night Dream*?" The old-timer was English. Undoubtedly a Geordie, most likely from Tyneside, Kirk surmised, judging by the way the miner had said, "fool."

"I'm afraid I wasn't listening." Kirk wasn't surprised that the miners were debating Elizabethan literature. Harsh western winters left pioneers with plenty of time to read between October and April, and it was the odd frontiersmen who couldn't hold his own when it came to discussing topics ranging from mathematics to philosophy. What was surprising was just how fervently these sourdoughs felt about this riddle.

"Ya talk like a canny lad too! Surely someone who's been educated must ha' an opinion on the subject!"

Honestly, Kirk didn't. As far as he was concerned, the play was the thing. It didn't matter to

Kirk who wrote *Macbeth* anymore than *Our American Cousin*, but he doubted the prickly miners wanted to hear that. Diplomacy seemed to be his best course of action. "Well," he began, "I would have to say that the people making the claim for Bacon have to at least establish a *prima facie* case against Shakespeare's authorship. Until then—"

"We did!" the big miner interrupted, loud enough to quiet the saloon. "Let me give you one for-instance. You sound like you might know the law, sir. So, if you've read the plays that some claim were written by Shakespeare, then you can't deny that the playwright was as smart as a tree full of owls when it came to the law."

Kirk could not disagree.

"Now, I ask you, how could some rustic who started off holding horses in front of theaters as a boy know the law that well?"

As much as Kirk wanted to remain diplomatic, he couldn't stop himself from rising to the bait. "If that's true, how could we be having this discussion?"

"I don't follow you."

"Let me give *you* a for-instance. Take President Lincoln. He was more book-learned than schooled, as I'd guess most of us here are; yet he not only became a lawyer, but an outstanding thinker and writer. If a boy from Kentucky could do that, why not one from Stratford-upon-Avon?"

The big miner could not deny that Kirk could be right. But he wasn't happy about it. Not at all.

"So!" the graybeard chuckled. "Ya do agree that Bacon couldn't be Shakespeare!"

Oh-oh, thought Kirk. He could have kicked himself. *Why can't you learn to keep your nose in your own book?* Now Kirk had to say something to appease all the miners or risk offending some of these men and becoming the cause of a shindy, if not an out-and-out brawl.

"The truth is, I don't believe Bacon wrote the works of Shakespeare."

This sent a ripple of discontent through the saloon.

"But I also don't believe Shakespeare wrote them either."

More ripples. A heap of ripples.

"What I really think happened is that the works attributed to Shakespeare were written by someone else . . . but someone with the same name."

The ripples faded into stunned silence. Then the saloon erupted into laughter.

As the music started again and folks got back to whatever they had been doing, the big miner reached out to shake Kirk's hand. "You're a pip, sir! My name's Linus Grimm. Glad to meet you."

"Paul Kirk." He shook hands with Grimm and tried not to wince when the miner squeezed.

The graybeard reached out to shake hands next. "Abe Stoker. For once I ha' ta agree w' Linus, Mr. Kirk. Ya are a reet mazer!"

"Thank you, Mr. Stoker. Are you fellows working the Ute-Ulay mine or are you with the Ocean Wave group?"

"The Golden Fleece. If ya don't mind me sayin', lad, ya look like some sorta manhunter."

"I am. I just rode in from Eleanor."

"Surely? Come lookin' for Colorow, eh?

"No, sir."

"Oh? Such a pity."

"Yes. I've heard how some White River renegades are giving you folks trouble."

Stoker made an act of thinking. "What's it been, Linus? Two weeks or three since those Utes surrounded Lake City?"

"Two and a half, Abraham. Mr. Kirk, it didn't look good. Mothers were hiding their children in the attic and passing them shotguns by the time Chief Ouray got wind of our predicament. He rode over from the Los Pinos Agency just in time to convince the renegades to simmer down."

"He wa' certainly the white man's friend that day," Stoker added. "It's jus' one more thing that we're beholdin' to the Chief."

The other miners listening to the conversation said, "Amen."

"Even so," Kirk asked, "why did you think I would be looking for Colorow? Didn't the Army send him to the Unitah Reservation last fall?"

Grimm said, "They did, but Colorow swore then that he'd come back to hunt elk and deer in his Shining Mountains every winter. And enough of us saw him during the last snows that I can promise you he kept his word. And I can promise you he's around here now, likely stirring things up, for the same reason. It seems that the only folks who haven't seen Colorow lately are the blue bellies!"

Kirk nodded. "I'm sorry to hear that."

"So what does bring you to Lake City, Mr. Kirk? We've no desperados."

"I was hired by the Nox Syndicate to track down the cross killers."

Grimm tipped his mug of beer to Kirk. "Yes, we heard about Jon Brand. I wish you luck, but why come to Lake City? Those dry-gulchers haven't waylaid anyone in these parts going on three years now."

"I wanted to read what the *Silver World* had written about them, and one of Dave Cook's men has agreed to show me around one of the bush-whacker's kill sites near here."

Stoker suggested, "It could be ye'r lookin' for Colorow but don't know it. Plenty of us think he and his renegades killed all those poor folks."

Kirk still doubted that any Indian, including Colorow, was responsible for the bushwhackings, but preferred to say nothing and learn what he could from the miners.

A third sourdough at the bar spoke up: "If'n Colorow is or he ain't behind 'em, he's getting his bunch ready to go on the war-path soon. Never mind them surrounding Lake City the way they just did. Can anyone recollect the last time any of them White River braves took anything 'cept ammunition in trade for furs? I say God bless Chief Ouray for keeping them renegades in line as long as he has, but even Joan of Arc couldn't save France on her own, if you know what I mean."

"Right you are, Quincy," Grimm agreed. Turning to Kirk, he said, "Let me ask, did you happen to see any sign of Utes near Lake City on your way into town?"

"I spotted some travois tracks this afternoon."

"Where?"

"About six miles south of here. I didn't want any trouble to slow me down, so I gave the tracks a wide berth."

"You see! With the Los Pinos Agency north of us, no law-abiding Ute has any business being where you saw those tracks! The only Utes who would have made them would be Colorow's renegades."

Kirk nodded again. "You fellows present me with a problem. It doesn't pay in my profession to ignore any possibilities, but Colorow would be harder than Dave Rudabaugh to find and question."

Grimm and Stoker exchanged looks, then faced Kirk. The graybeard said, "If ye'r serious 'bout wantin' to talk with Colorow, we can tell ya how ta find him."

"You know where he is?"

"No. Oh, it's no secret Colorow's fond of some cave near here. Jus' nobody knows where 'tis exactly! But, if ya ha' the patience and ye'r willin' ta put yer neck on the block, ya can get Colorow ta come ta ya."

"How?"

Grimm smirked. "You know the chestnut about catching flies with honey? Well, as more than one poor woman in these parts has found out, to get Colorow's attention, all you need is a baking pan, flour, and syrup."

The next morning Kirk was up with the chickens, baking biscuits.

He had built a scrub oak fire five miles east of Lake City, on a bluff at the southern end of Slumgullion Pass called Cannibal Plateau. Except for his grulla, Kirk's only companions were the gravestones of five prospectors who got lost in the winter of 1873 and were murdered by the sixth member of their party, the infamous Alferd Packer.

Mixing a batch of dough, Kirk put a pan of biscuits over the fire, then sat down and waited for them to cook. To pass the time, he read *Hamlet*, borrowed from Grimm.

Kirk had originally considered setting up his camp where he had spotted the travois tracks. That was right after Grimm and Stoker explained to him how Colorow couldn't resist biscuits. "The man wa' already six feet tall, but he mus' weigh two-seventy-five now thanks to that appetite o' his!" Stoker told Kirk. All summer Colorow had made a frightening nuisance of himself by poking his head into the window of any cabin where he smelled someone baking biscuits.

Grimm told Kirk, "The man simply can't get enough of them! Especially with syrup! Colorow will barge in and eat biscuits until his host runs out of flour. Then he calls his braves, and they'll bring more flour. It'd be humorous if the poor women he's intruded on weren't shaken to their wits."

It was while Kirk was riding out of Lake City that morning that he spotted Slumgullion Pass in the distance and reconsidered his destination. Cannibal Plateau was a mile higher in elevation than Lake City, and it was possible that Colorow, having surrounded the town once, might be keeping an outlook or two in reserve on or near the bluff. Besides that, Cannibal Plateau was isolated. There were snow-capped peaks on all sides of

Slumgullion Pass, and a ring of aspens, pines, and scrub oaks encompassed the bluff. All in all, Cannibal Plateau was an unique locale: an adequate spot to hide, yet, for his purposes, an excellent place to be seen.

Kirk's first batch of biscuits was done. As he set to work baking a second batch, he shook his head. "I guess even Achilles had his heel."

Hours passed as the sun climbed higher above the peaks, but Kirk had fished enough to know that patience was the key to success. He also hadn't spotted a red fox or weasel for several minutes, and the jays and nuthatches had stopped their usual chattering. Kirk suspected he had a nibble.

Not long after his suspicions were proved right when a dozen or so braves stepped out in front of the bluff's trees. As they stood sentry, a Ute riding a buckskin horse with a willow tail came out of an aspen grove. He was large, like Grimm and Stoker had described Colorow, and intimidating, with a single-barrel shotgun cradled in his arms. The Ute didn't bother to glance at the prospectors' graves as he went by them, keeping his eyes on Kirk while maintaining a slow, inevitable pace, like Death preceding a banshee's wail. The Ute finally stopped a few yards from the scrub oak fire.

"Colorow?" Kirk acted composed, but it was just that—an act. He couldn't remember being this scared since Murfreesboro.

The Ute nodded once.

"My name is Paul Kirk." He knew Colorow spoke English. That the Indian had even worked as a translator for the Army long ago. But Kirk wanted to show his respect, so he spoke in the Ute language. "I wasn't sure you would come talk to me."

Colorow wasn't impressed. In English, "Many eyes watch you." This wasn't intended as a threat. Colorow was merely stating a fact.

"I only wanted to ask you about the cross killers. Are you familiar with that name?"

"I know it. I know many whites think Utes do these killings. We do not."

"I did not think so."

Colorow looked at Kirk for several seconds. Neither man blinked or showed any emotion. Kirk didn't even breathe, until Colorow said, "We talk." The Ute dismounted and sat down across the cook fire form Kirk.

Kirk opened a jug of syrup and brought it along with a pan of biscuits to the Ute.

Colorow poured the syrup over the biscuits and commenced eating. Between bites he asked Kirk, "Why talk to me? Why risk your life?"

"I need to find the cross killers."

"Why? For money?"

"They killed my sister's son."

Colorow stopped eating for a minute, perhaps to chew on Kirk's answer instead. Finally, he began eating again. "What do you think I know about cross killers?"

"I got to thinking that you, or your braves, might have seen something of the cross killers while in these mountains."

"I see nothing. Utes see nothing. Cross killers leave no tracks. Leave no sign of camps. They kill no Indians. We don't know why."

"Do you have a guess who they may be? Where they could be hiding out?"

"No. No."

"I see." Kirk tried not to show his disappointment. He knew he had been playing a long shot, after all.

Colorow finished the biscuits. "Why do you think I am not a cross killer?"

"Because you fight with honor."

"I kill white men. Can kill you."

Kirk tried not to dwell on the latter. "You have never attacked a miner's or settler's cabin without warning them first to pack up and go."

"Most leave." Colorow smiled.

"Even though the Army sent you away from here because of the Meeker massacre, everything I've read about that attack tells me you had nothing to do with it."

"Some say I order attack on the White River Agency."

"Well, some say you surrounded Lake City a few weeks ago. If you did, why didn't you wipe it out like the Agency when you had the chance? I suppose it could be you just wanted to scare off the folks living there."

Colorow said nothing.

"It was the miners in Lake City who told me how you've been getting biscuits from settler women. Women who are your enemy and were at your mercy. Yet you have never harmed one of them."

Colorow stared at Kirk, then stood, walked around the fire, and handed Kirk the empty pan.

"I do guess one thing about cross killers. Maybe you guess it too."

"What?"

"Men who can hide and kill like them are crazy, but are most dangerous because they don't know they crazy."

Kirk watched as Colorow turned around and walked to the buckskin.

"Now do this favor for me, Paul Kirk. Tell men in Lake City that Colorow leave his Shining Mountains for a short time. That a time has come that he must go west." Mounting the horse, the Ute started riding away at the same pace he had entered camp. Without bothering to look at Kirk again, he added, "But I come back. I always come back."

CHAPTER NINE

"Morning, John."

John Lieninger, proprietor of Eleanor's Book & Stationery, stiffened as Moses entered his shop. Gregory Musgrove and Tim Duggan did likewise. Musgrove worked next door as a loan officer. Duggan had his own tailor shop a block south on Aspen Lane. All three men were officers in Eleanor's Committee for Citizens' Protection.

"Morning, Sheriff," was the general reply from all three.

"Boys, I'll come straight to the point. You're wrong if you think I don't know what goes on in this town."

The men looked innocent. Or tried to, anyway.

"Thanks to Teddy shooting off his mouth, Eleanor's had two days to worry itself into believing ten thousand Utes or Rapahoes are skulking out on the tableland."

"Your deputy *did* see an Indian out where Jon Brand was killed," Musgrove challenged.

"My deputy *thinks* he saw an Indian wearing white man's clothes, so if he really saw someone, I doubt it was a renegade. In any case, even if Teddy did see an Indian, that's a mighty slim reason for you vigilantes to get worked up over."

The three men reacted as if they had never heard the word vigilante in their lives.

"Oh, shut your pie-holes! Your committee has behaved itself since attending to Sheriff Morris' killers. You've left me alone, so I've left you alone. So help me, though, if one of you even whispers that the time has come to start stringing up Indians from the Argos bridge for whatever reason, I'll toss you all into the hoosegow."

Seeing they were licked, Lieninger said, "You can't deny that renegades are a real threat. They've murdered settlers, attacked small communities, and last year . . ."

"All that was up around Middle Park. Nobody's seen a renegade further than half a day from Lake City. Trust me, I'd know if any Utes or Rapahoes were near Eleanor."

"Why should we trust you about Indians?" Duggan wanted to know. "You haven't even found a trace of the cross killers in over three years."

The sheriff looked at Duggan with a less than pleasant expression.

"He didn't mean it, Moses," Lieninger piped up. "He wasn't thinking."

"None of you are thinking, John. That's my problem."

A ten-year-old boy, Dean Ehlinger, entered the shop as Lieninger insisted, "We only want to protect our families. We have to be prepared in case."

Dean, not sure if he was doing the right thing, tugged on Moses' sleeve. "Sheriff? Mr. Cully says you got a message down at the telegraph office. Says you wanted to know right away if you got this one."

"Thanks." Then, staring at Duggan, he said, "I don't care a Continental if you trust me or not, Tim. I will not tolerate anyone giving townsfolk the vapors over some phantom Indian."

Moses led Dean outside. When the shop's door closed, the vigilantes started breathing again.

A minute later the sheriff and boy stepped into the telegraph office, its door standing open. Cully MacDonald, the telegrapher, handed a message to Moses. "This just came through."

The War Department was answering a query from the sheriff about Kirk. Moses read it, then, "Is this all?"

"That's all."

Moses considered what he could do next. "Cully, send a message to the sheriff in Leadville. Tell him I'd like to talk with a miner named Artemus Hawley. He was working at the Gone-Abroad last I heard. I need Artemus brought to a telegraph office quick so I can ask him some questions directly about a Union prisoner named Paul Kirk. Fetch me as soon as all that's done."

"Yes, sir." As Cully went to work, Moses' message started playing over the telegraph in the Nox office, which shared lines with the town.

"Paul Kirk again?" Hasek commented to a clerk working with him.

"What's up?"

"Sheriff Moses wants to talk to a rocker at the Gone-Abroad about Kirk." The Gone-Abroad was one of two Leadville mines, along with the Small Hope, owned by the Nox syndicate. "Maybe Mr. Brand should know. Kirk's working for him, and Sheriff Moses wants to talk to one of our miners."

"Maybe he should."

Hasek grabbed his hat. "I'll ride up to the bluff and tell him. Be right back."

"A couple of '59ers came across the body right there."

Bob Harker, a civilian member of Cook's Rocky Mountain Detective Association, pointed to a low divide between two depressions.

"In those willows?" Kirk asked. He and Harker were less than twenty paces away, standing with their horses under the shelter of a ridge.

Harker, gnarly as a wind timber, removed his broad-brimmed beaver hat to swat bees from his face. "They was afraid he might be on the shoot, but when they spotted his boots and noticed he weren't moving, they reckoned he were a white man and a dead one at that."

A woodpecker popped away in a nearby ravine as Kirk studied the sad scene. Wild roses were in bloom, and their heady fragrance prevailed over the piquant odor of hundreds of conifers scattered in copses about the divide. "Plenty of places for an assassin to lay in ambush."

"The dead man was a rocker named Guy O'Connor. Mined these parts since '63, so the Long Toms who found him recognized him right off and fetched me."

"That was on August 14, 1876?"

"Yea." Harker also confirmed that he had searched every tuft of grass that day. "I didn't find a horse track or any empty shells, and O'Connor weren't robbed and still had his hair. So a fight didn't kill him, and it weren't the work of road agents or Indians."

Kirk ambled towards the willows. "O'Connor was shot in the center of his forehead?"

"Smack dab." Harker followed, putting on his hat so he could carry his Big Fifty Hawkins in both hands.

"Would you say the bushwhackers fired from that spot?" Kirk pointed to an oak coppice fifty yards from the willows.

"Most likely. Not a far shot but it weren't easy, what with all them trees in the way."

Kirk stared where O'Connor, first victim of the "cross killers," had fallen.

"What reason did those hard cases have for killing O'Connor?" Harker spat. "None, 'cept sheer cussedness. Then they kill two more men below Slumgullion Pass and another near South Fork on the same day for no better reason! With those crosses carved in O'Connor and them others, everyone in these parts knew this were the work of one man or gang. I ain't ever heard the like before! It's crazy! Plumb crazy!"

Kirk remembered Colorow's guess. "Crazy, yes, but there's some sort of method to this madness."

"You think they did have a reason for killing O'Connor?"

"Men who kill as slick as this never commit to a campaign without some sort of cause. Even a lunatic one. I only wish I knew what it was."

Stepping from under the willows, Kirk scanned the distance where snow-capped peaks rose above the divide in all four directions.

"Four men killed in one day," he thought out loud. "First O'Connor, then Dlouhy and Bennett nearly twenty miles away, then Sanders over twice that distance again. What was their hurry?"

"Well, maybe they was trying to get everyone's attention, for whatever reason they do have. Four dead in one day did that, I reckon."

An idea struck Kirk like an epiphany. "What do you mean, 'everyone'?"

Harker did not understand.

"Whose attention were the bushwhackers trying to get?"

"Like I said: '*everyone's.*' Everyone in the San Juans, at least."

"No! Not just the San Juans. Think about it, Mr. Harker. Thanks to the crosses carved in their victims' chests, news of any fresh bushwhackings by this gang spreads like wildfire across Colorado."

Harker supposed Kirk was correct. "So?" he asked.

"A journalist and I were discussing these murders a couple of days ago, and I told him the bushwhackers have been choosing victims at random. I'll have to modify that."

Cook's man was feeling more confused by the second. "Pardon?"

"What's the one thing all twenty-seven victims have in common?"

" 'Sides all being God's creatures? Nothing."

Kirk shook his head. "They've all been killed in Colorado."

Harker did not waste breath saying that was obvious.

"Why haven't there been any bushwhackings in the New Mexico territory? Or the Arizona and Utah territories? Why not, when they'll travel nearly one hundred miles in a single day to kill four people?"

"That's a point," Harker admitted.

"There must be a reason why the bushwhackers haven't killed anyone anywhere except in Colorado." Kirk rummaged his memory for every scrap of information he had read about the twenty-seven murders, and, somewhere along the line, another idea struck hard. Rushing back to the ridge, he untied a saddle bag and pulled out a battered old family Bible, inside which he had tucked his *Epitaph* notes for safekeeping. Searching through them, he slapped his forehead. "Now I know how Ned felt."

Harker followed Kirk. "What's it now?"

"Does the date August 14, 1876, mean anything to you? Besides being the day O'Connor was killed?" Harker could not think of any significance. "How about August 1, 1876?"

"That's Statehood Day! No Coloradoan will say different!"

"And precisely a fortnight later, O'Connor, Dlouhy, Bennett, and Sanders were all killed."

What Kirk was suggesting seemed far-fetched to

Harker. "People are getting butchered because we became a state?"

"Look here." Kirk showed his notes to Harker and pointed to a list of the twenty-seven victims along with the dates their bodies were discovered. "Hal Wright was found dead near Silverton on the morning of August 2, 1877. On the afternoon of August 9, 1878, the bodies of B.F. and Karen Hilderbrand were found along Wolf Creek Pass."

"Okay—so?"

Kirk pointed to another page. "Here! According to the coroner who examined Wright, the victim had been dead less than twenty-four hours. The Hilderbrands' coroner, meanwhile, testified that the couple had been dead a little over a week." He tapped the victims' list with an index finger. "Wright very likely was murdered on August 1, 1877, while it's probable that the Hilderbrands were murdered one year later. If that's correct, then August first is the only constant date the bushwhackers have struck on since 1876. This *can't* be just coinci—"

The *sizzle* of a rattlesnake's tail interrupted Kirk.

The men turned towards the base of a juniper pine, where a long-tailed roadrunner was attacking the rattler, apparently for no more cause than the pure joy of killing the reptile.

"I can't believe it's merely a coincidence." Kirk's voice was hushed, almost reverential. "I won't."

CHAPTER TEN

Joshua charged into the sheriff's office. "Where's Moses?"

Coleman pointed towards the west end of town. "At your office, Mr. Brand."

"What's wrong at the Nox?"

"Nothing I know of, sir. The sheriff sent the Ehlinger boy over a few minutes ago to tell me he was meeting you at your office."

This made no sense to Joshua. What was Moses up to? "If he returns without my seeing him, you tell him to stay put, unless he's grown tired of being sheriff."

Going back across the Tansey, Joshua entered the Nox Building. "Is Sheriff Moses here?"

"Upstairs, sir."

Sure enough, Moses was patiently waiting on the second floor, alone, at the telegrapher's table. "Morning, Josh."

"Where is everyone?"

"Having an early lunch. I figured you and I should hash this out between us."

"Hash what out? What are you doing here?"

"You know about the telegraph I sent to Lake City."

It did not slip Joshua's attention that Moses had not asked a question. "Of course."

"And the one I sent to the War Department about Paul Kirk."

"And their answer: Kirk was taken to Salisbury Prison after Murfreesboro, where he spent the remainder of the war. All you had to do was ask me and I could have told you that."

"Could have told me, sure. Would have? I ain't so sure."

That bordered on calling Joshua a liar, something Brand did not appreciate.

"Why didn't you just tell me, Josh? Were you hoping the War Department maybe wouldn't answer my telegram?"

"Honestly? I didn't want to bother with it."

Moses could have snorted. "You do now, though, huh?"

"I'm bothered that you seem unsatisfied with what the War Department has told you. Now you're dragging one of my employees away from his job. And why? So you can question him regarding someone you shouldn't be concerned about one whit."

"Honestly? I am concerned, especially after what Ella said the other night."

"She's distraught!" Brand shouted. "Jeb, we've lost our son!"

"I know! I brought the boy home, remember?

I'm more sorry about Jon than I can say, but twenty-six others are dead too! Not a one of these other folks deserved to die any more than Jon did, and I don't want there to be any more like them!"

Joshua found that an acceptable point of view. "So why do you think this miner knows anything more about Paul Kirk than the War Department?"

"I don't. I do know, however, that Artemus Hawley served sentinel duty at Salisbury until sometime in 1864. I'm hoping he remembers Kirk, and, if he does, might recall the kind of prisoner Kirk was. You can tell an awful lot about a man's character when the chips are down, and I don't imagine life can get much worse than when you're a prisoner of war."

"You're searching for some sort of character reference?"

"From an impartial observer. Yes."

Shaking his head, "I don't claim to understand it, but if this will satisfy you, then fine. Shouldn't we get Ondrej up here?"

"Why? I said we ought to keep this between us."

"You don't expect me to operate that telegraph?"

"I'll do it."

Joshua was amazed that Moses knew Morse.

Moses was, in turn, amazed at Joshua's amazement. "Even outlaws got to keep up with the times," he said. "What sense does it make to tap a telegraph wire if you can't understand what you're listening to?"

Joshua confessed he had never given that much thought, but added, "What does all this privacy matter when MacDonald's going to hear everything anyway?"

"Cully came down with a dry gullet, so I told him to go cut the dust from his throat while I covered for him up here. Knowing Cully, I wouldn't be surprised if he didn't lock his office and maybe even disconnect his telegraph before he left." Moses grinned.

Eleanor's leading citizen scrunched his brow. "Seems you're a popular man in our town."

"Don't get your knickers in a knot. Cully did it for you as much as me. I can't vouch for Artemus or the sheriff and telegrapher at Lake City. Kirk means nothing to them, though, so I suspect they won't be jawing about this. At least not to anyone that matters to us." Moses leveled at Joshua. "Unless, I suppose, Artemus knows something suspicious about Kirk and they all start wondering why I'm asking about him."

"You're speaking particularly free with me, Jeb."

"I'll talk any way I choose, Josh. Give Teddy my badge if you don't like it."

Despite what Joshua had warned Coleman, firing the best sheriff in Eleanor's history did not appeal to him. He took a seat.

Seven minutes later Hawley signaled he was ready to talk with Moses. Joshua listened in on their *dots* and *dashes*:

MOSES: *DO YOU REMEMBER A PRISONER NAMED PAUL KIRK?*

HAWLEY: *YES.*

MOSES: *WAS HE ANY TROUBLE TO YOU?*

HAWLEY: *HE WAS FINE FOR AS LONG AS HE WAS THERE.*

Moses glanced at Joshua. "What do you think

that means, 'As long as he was there'?" Joshua shrugged as if he had no idea.

MOSES: *HOW LONG WAS HE THERE?*

HAWLEY: *ARRIVED JANUARY 1863. ESCAPED OCTOBER 1863.*

Moses sucked on his teeth, contemplating, then asked Hawley if he was certain Kirk had escaped. Hawley replied that not many men escaped from Salisbury during his tour of duty, so it was no trick to recall Kirk.

"I suppose you didn't know Kirk escaped?" the sheriff asked Joshua while tapping his thanks to the miner.

"No. The only reason I even knew Paul was still alive was because I spotted his name and our company on an old prisoners list after the war."

"You knew he worked for Pinkerton's too."

Joshua scowled. "Are you going to tell me you never heard of Paul Kirk before last week? Even without a yellowback dedicated to his exploits, Paul's earned quite a reputation. Knowing him as I did from childhood, it wasn't hard for me to deduce that my brother-in-law and Pinkerton's Paul Kirk had to be one and the same."

"So the War Department puts Kirk's name on a prisoner of war list, but they didn't know about him escaping?"

"War records are notoriously incomplete. It's possible news of his escape was lost or never even reached the War Department."

Moses confessed that could very well have been the case. "I guess I'll have to ask Kirk his opinion about this, if he ever gets back from his gallivanting."

"He'll be back. Have no doubts."

"Want to know what he tells me when I ask him?"

"What do you think?"

"Just offering." Moses stood. "I best tell Cully and Ondrej they can mosey back to work." Next, he started for the stairs, then stopped. "Mind my asking how come you and Kirk never patched things up? Knowing him the way you did from childhood and all."

Joshua glared at the telegraph with no intention of looking at Moses. After a few seconds the sheriff walked down the steps.

As soon as the AT&SF train from Dodge City pulled into the Pueblo depot, Thompson's detachment was informed that Captain Webb and his men were holed up in the Denver and Rio Grande's roundhouse.

"Word arrived last night that the Supreme Court has awarded control of the Royal Gorge trestle back to General Palmer and the D&RG. Palmer's been trying to coax our boys out of the roundhouse ever since with a bribe."

"So what does Captain Webb want us to do? Join him or wait?" asked Thompson.

"Neither. Palmer is preoccupied with the roundhouse. He has no idea you boys are here. So Captain Webb figures we can counterstrike if you all saddle up right now and secure the pass down at Trinidad."

Thompson liked the plan, but many of his men immediately made it clear that they intended to remain in Pueblo, hoping to get a cut of the D&RG's tribute. Thompson told them, "Any of you want to stay and risk receiving any pay from the Santa Fe, I can't stop you, but I'm leaving in five minutes."

Bartholomew Fairchild had no idea what to do. Fighting for the railroad at Cañon City was one thing. Following Thompson south meant abandoning Kathryn and Penny in Pueblo, where the Coloradoans might figure out he had gone off to fight for the rival Kansas railroad and take it out on his family.

He looked at Kathryn, who counseled, "You do what you think is best."

Penny added, "Mama's right, Papa. I won't retract what I said before, but I don't want the past to continue haunting you either. If going with Mr. Thompson is the only way you can find peace, then go."

Bartholomew could hardly breathe. He knew his wife and daughter were aware of the hardships his going could cause them, yet they still thought of him first. *Maybe I don't deserve you or your mother either, child.* Instead, he said, "We have tickets for Cañon City, and that's where we're going."

The women asked if Bartholomew knew what he'd just said.

"Of course. I doubt we'll be welcome in Cañon City, but they have a stage that goes to Lake City. There we can buy two wagons and follow the Cinnamon Pass to Eleanor. I hear it's a fine town, and should be far enough west that I suspect its citizens wouldn't hold my signing with the AT&SF against me. If we like Eleanor, we can winter there. If we don't, I hear California is the place to be, so maybe we'll continue on to San Francisco. What do you think, Sunflower?"

"I think that sounds fine, Papa." Penny could not have felt happier as her mother squeezed Bartholomew's hand.

Bartholomew informed Thompson of his decision, the men shook hands, and then, soon, the Fairchilds were sitting by themselves in the car. He was doing the right thing. He knew it, or prayed he would come to know it in time.

Waiting for the train to begin the final leg of its journey, the women in his life chattering with plans, Bartholomew stared out his window and imagined what must be going on at the D&RG's roundhouse. The building probably looked like most roundhouses, built of brick with timber roof framing, and with something like ten stalls for the locomotives. Palmer and his guards had to be standing vigil around it and its turntable, while inside, Webb and his gunmen would be passing time in the deep floor pits of the service stalls. Those stalls would make wonderful trenches in case Palmer ordered a charge.

We could have used pits like that at Culpepper. They certainly would have been more useful than benches and counters.

The train whistle wailed, the Pullman car lurched as if tugged by Jehovah's own hand, and the Fairchilds were on their way again, two of them grateful to be leaving the village behind.

CHAPTER ELEVEN

Trail-weary and grubby, Kirk, riding down Argos Avenue, spotted one of his father's old friends, Amory Catinat.

"Howdy, Mr. Figaro!"

Catinat, a Canadian and the great-grandson of Huguenot immigrants, was a well-groomed man of sixty who walked with a graceful carriage for a man his age. He went on walking down the sidewalk a few steps after Kirk's greeting then slowed, as if thinking he could not have heard right. Stopping, Catinat turned with the dread of the Ancient Mariner.

"Paul Kirk?"

"How long has it been since anyone's called you 'Mr. Figaro,' Monsieur Catinat?"

"I thought I heard you were resurrected, little Kirk. Too bad God didn't offer you the choice to remain dead."

"Pardon me?"

Once upon a time Catinat, the town barber, had cut Kirk's hair while singing opera in a beautiful *basso profundo*. Catinat's favorite opera was *The Barber of Seville*—hence "Mr. Figaro"—but the barber often sang *The Magic Flute* while cutting young Kirk's hair because Amos' son loved it so. As a boy Kirk thought a chair in Catinat's shop was better than a box seat at *Teatro alla Scala*.

"You heard me." So did a handful of pedestrians, a few who realized they recognized the rider and stopped to gawk.

Kirk, feeling like a parakeet in a cage, told Catinat, "Sorry you feel that way, sir," then rode away before he said something he could expect to regret another day.

At the jailhouse, Kirk slapped the dust off his clothes before he entered. Inside he found Moses talking sternly to Coleman, but the sheriff stopped when he noticed Kirk. "Hello," he said.

"You look like a man who can use a drink." Moses offered the manhunter some coffee.

"I'd appreciate it. Thank you." A healthy sip made Kirk feel a bit sprier. "Has anything happened? You two sounded pretty serious."

Moses intended to ask about Salisbury Prison after explaining, "My deputy and I were discussing a pow-wow I had a few days ago with Eleanor's Committee for Citizens' Protection. They're spooked because Teddy thinks he saw an Indian out on the tableland right after you rode off for Lake City."

Kirk stopped sipping.

Moses forgot about Salisbury. "That mean something to you?"

"What did this Indian look like?"

"Teddy claims he was wearing white man's duds and holding a large rifle. Why?"

Setting his coffee on the sheriff's desk, Kirk rubbed the back of his neck like a man who just wanted to get some sleep. "I know him. His name's Mudeater. I call him Muddy. Seems more polite."

"There *is* an Indian out there?" Coleman asked excitedly. "No fooling?" The deputy felt like whooping, until he noticed Moses glaring at him.

The sheriff asked Kirk, "What's this Mudeater doing out there?"

"Trying not to be seen, for one thing. You'd do a hawk proud, deputy."

"I only glimpsed him."

"That's more than most see of Muddy when he's on the trail."

Moses asked, "Trailing who? The cross killers?"

"Yes, sir. Muddy's a Pinkerton, like me, and a government scout. When we got here we had no idea when or, for that matter, where the bushwhackers would strike again. Since Eleanor has been at the hub of their activity, we decided Muddy should scrounge for any kind of trail in this vicinity while keeping one eye open in case the bushwhackers returned. That would leave me free to research and take care of any associated matters. It seemed like the most productive gamble at the time."

Coleman snapped his fingers. "He's sort of an ace in the hole."

"Exactly."

Moses told Kirk, "Bring him into town."

"Now, Sheriff . . ."

"Yes, *now*, Mr. Kirk. I want people—particularly our upstanding vigilantes—to see that this Mudeater ain't some sort of renegade before they lynch some passing Ute, Rapahoe, or Cheyenne. Have you any notion the bloodshed that would cause?"

Kirk did. "You're right. I'll fetch him."

"And I'll go with you." Moses instructed Coleman, "Mind the store. Oh, and Teddy, if you get the chance, spread the word who your Indian turned out to be."

Moses nodded and procured one Winchester from the rifle rack, double-checked to make sure it was loaded, and followed Kirk to their horses.

"This will do," Kirk said, parking his grulla a half-mile out of town. Tipping his hat so the brim blocked the sun from his face, he closed his eyes and bowed his back to relax.

"You going to sleep on me?"

"I'm tired, Sheriff. Being in the saddle for the better part of four days does that to a man."

"I want that Indian here! Now!"

"I know. He'll be here."

"When?"

"First he has to see us, which shouldn't take long. He probably already has, but he's riding shank's mare and it may take him a while to reach us on foot."

The bigger man swept the wide tableland with his eyes. "Can't you signal him somehow?"

In a testy voice, Kirk asked, "You mean besides sitting out here in the open where a shave tail could spot us?"

"Watch your mouth. You ain't the only one who's short on patience today."

Kirk ignored Moses, closing his eyes and slumping in his saddle again.

With nothing better to do Moses continued to sweep the area until, almost twenty minutes later, a man materialized less than ten yards leeward.

"Afternoon to you, Sheriff Moses. An honor to meet you."

Where in the world? "Mudeater?"

"Call me Muddy. Most white folks seem to prefer it."

Mudeater appeared to be a self-assured man somewhere around fifty, with a square body to match his square head. He wore a cloth shirt, buckskin breeches, a large hat, and cavalry boots. A double rifle-shotgun scabbard, packed with a Colt double barrel and a Sharps military rifle, was slung across his back and a longhorn hung about his waist in a Huckleberry rig. Around his thick wrists were cuffs with "U.S." inlays. His emerald green eyes, sparkling with mirth, and his voice, warm as a favorite aunt's, contrasted with his appearance, which was as weathered and reflective as Uncompahgre Peak.

Moses told Kirk, "Your friend's here." But Kirk did not stir. "Kirk?" He nudged the manhunter, but Kirk would not respond. "Just my luck. He died."

"Naw," Mudeater laughed. "He's tuckered out, is all. Let him siesta some more and he'll be rear-ing to lead the cavalry. You must be a man to tie to, Sheriff. Paul trusts you."

"Pardon?"

Muddy petted the grulla's nose. "Paul sleeps light like a cat unless he's sure someone reliable is on watch." Mudeater gave Kirk a good-natured shove, and Kirk instinctively righted himself before falling out of the saddle. Barely awake, Kirk mumbled, "Ella?"

"Just me, old son." He climbed up behind Kirk's saddle and took the reins. "I'll take us in." To Moses, he asked, "You do want me to come into town and let folks know there're no Utes out here?"

"How'd you know that?"

"I've come in a time or two while Paul was away. Heard folks talk. It isn't hard to guess why you two wanted to find me."

"All right. Have you seen any Utes?"

"Not a one." Then, with a smile, "Not yet, anyway." Mudeater turned the grulla around and the men rode into town.

The sun danced on the crests of the San Juans as the sheriff and manhunters rode up to the Galena.

"Siesta's over," Moses informed Mudeater. "I think some grub will do us all good."

Mudeater roused his friend and the three men went inside, where their arrival had the same effect on the noisy supper crowd as a minister approaching a pulpit.

"Evening, folks," Moses greeted, happy to have everyone's attention. Loudly, "Most of you already know Mr. Kirk. I'd like you to meet a friend of his. Say howdy to the people, Mr. Mudeater."

Kirk wanted to hide under a rock, but Mudeater seemed delighted by their predicament. Smiling, he bellowed like a candidate for governor, "Hello, everyone! It's a pleasure! An honest pleasure!"

"This gentleman is the same Indian that Teddy saw out on the tableland. As you can see, Mr. Mudeater ain't a Ute or Rapahoe, and, if my opinion means anything, he strikes me as something less than a renegade."

"Anything but," Mudeater added. "I've reconnoitered quite a bit of the territory around Eleanor for nearly a week now, and if it can ease your minds some, let me assure you that I saw no hostile Indians in this locality."

The crowd listened. Kirk smirked. Moses had no idea what to make of Mudeater. Finally, the sheriff said, "Thank you."

"Certainly. Can I be of any further service?"

Moses shook his head.

"Fine. Paul? Let's eat!"

The manhunters moved to an empty table and started to ask Moses to join them when the Galena's proprietor, James Glidden, barked, "No Indians! And no dead men, for that matter!"

Mudeater informed Glidden, "I'm half white, sir."

"Half Indian makes you all Indian as far as the law and I are concerned."

"I'm the law, James." Moses pulled out a chair. "And the law wants you to serve us some grub."

The "dead man" wanted a hearty helping of beef, biscuits, gravy, potatoes, and greens. The "Indian" ordered grits with red-eye gravy. The "law" decided to have an antelope steak. The trio split a pot of coffee.

During their meal, Moses asked Mudeater, "You Sioux?"

"No. Cherokee and Irish."

"That beadwork on your belt is Sioux."

Mudeater nodded. "That it is. I'm very proud of it. A few years ago, before I met Paul, a Sioux chief and me had a *rencontre*. Things went my way and this belt is my trophy. Well, one of my trophies." He leered in a way to make a wise man nervous.

Moses was familiar with the wind-jamming of old men, but this tale did not strike him as a blow. If what Mudeater said was true, the half-breed was as formidable a man as Kirk.

Almost as if Kirk could read the sheriff's mind, he said, "Muddy taught me how to scout, how to track, even how to fight. At least in any way worth knowing."

"I wouldn't say that—you did all right before we hitched tandem, old son."

Moses asked, "How long have you two known each other?"

"We met during the war," Kirk answered.

"Before or after you escaped from Salisbury Prison?"

Neither manhunter stopped eating as Kirk asked, "How did you find out about that?"

"I wired the War Department about you. One of your old sentinels works in these parts, by the way. He said you were a fine prisoner. The queer thing is he says you escaped, but the War Department thinks you spent the war at Salisbury after you were captured."

"Hmm." Kirk went on eating.

"Mind telling me what you did after you escaped? I'm sure that don't fall under Pinkerton policy."

Mudeater coughed when he did not need to. "Paul doesn't like to talk about the war," he said.

"If you don't mind," Kirk added.

"Well, I do mind."

"Too bad."

Mudeater did not want to get caught between two big-horns butting heads. "Paul, the sheriff's doing his job. You can't fault him, what with your family history in Eleanor and how Brand hired you out of the blue and all."

"Why can't I fault him?" Kirk put his fork beside his plate. "What have I done that merits investigating? There's only one outlaw sitting at this table, and, oddly enough, he's the one collecting sheriff's wages."

Moses pushed his chair back from the table.

Kirk tossed a silver dollar in the sheriff's lap before Moses could stand.

"That'll cover supper." He told Mudeater, "I'm heading over to the Telluride. It's on Riffle Street, if you get the itch to join me."

Moses watched Kirk leave, then glared at Mudeater. "Why didn't you go with him?"

"Paul forgot I taught him never to leave a meal half-finished. We don't set out to starve none."

Bartholomew spotted an ideal camping ground across the Gunnison River an hour before sunset. The Fairchilds steered their wagons across to four acres of land cosseted within a horseshoe bend between the river's east bank and Lake San Cristobal. Parking their wagons across the bend's narrow neck, the family interlaced the wagon's tongues then set their horses free to feed.

Conies being abundant, Bartholomew plugged three through the eyes and gave them to Penny to dress. Laying the meat on a large flat stone, she beat it to a pulp using a smooth, smaller round rock. Kathryn did likewise with some mesquite beans she cooked over a fire made from buffalo chips, then mixed a third of the bean pulp with two-thirds meat pulp to form patties she fried in a skillet.

"Mother," Bartholomew crowed as he pitched a small watch tent by the wagons, "those meat patties smell better than one of Bat Masterson's prairie dogs."

"So do the buffalo chips," Penny groaned, getting a laugh out of her parents.

After supper the family spread blankets below the lee of the wagons, where Bartholomew cleaned his rifle. Penny unpacked her own shooting irons, knife, and whetstone, and took a seat beside him while Kathryn, the only child of a Kentucky mountain man and herb doctor, fried bannock for breakfast under the waning crescent moon. "This will taste good with that honey we purchased in Lake City."

Bartholomew laughed. "You'll have me fat as a banker if you keep cooking like this!" He glanced at the constellation Draco in the zone of midnight. "Mother, did you hear that talk back in Lake City about the Santa Fe selling lots?"

"Down near the Sangre de Cristo Range. Everyone was discussing it."

"I heard the place has already been laid out and the Santa Fe is calling it Cleora. If the Santa Fe ends up winning the right of way along the Arkansas to Leadville, Cleora might become something more than another terminus town. Maybe a respectable place like Denver."

Kathryn agreed, but Penny asked, "What happens if the D&RG secures the right of way?" It was a rhetorical question. Being long-time circuit peregrinators, they all knew that the D&RG would deny Cleora any assistance while laying out their own town a mile or two down the tracks—one that would not welcome a former Santa Fe janissary.

"The Santa Fe has the better gunmen," Penny deliberated, "but in the end this matter will have to be settled in court. Don't forget that the Supreme Court has just awarded the Royal Gorge trestle back to the D&RG."

Bartholomew sighed. "House odds don't seem to be in Cleora's favor, eh, Sunflower?"

"No, Papa."

"Then it's on to Eleanor for us. And from there, who knows?"

Kathryn advised, "Don't worry about that, Father. Tomorrow will bring what it brings." Penny seconded her mother as Bartholomew blew through the barrel of his rifle.

"I suppose it will," was all he said.

Their meal finished, Mudeater started for the Telluride.

The sheriff went with him, still intent on talking to Kirk. "He's had time to cool off."

"What about you?"

"What about me? I'm not the one who's been lying about my past."

"I've never known Paul to lie, and he sure didn't lie about his past or yours. You were an outlaw. I read where you held up the Nox stages so often that their horses responded better to your voice than any of the drivers!"

Now that is wind-jamming, thought Moses—though, to his sorrow, there was a grain of truth to it.

The two men turned right before crossing the Tansey. These three blocks, between the corner of Argos and the north end of Riffle where the original Nox reduction works still stood, were the riverfront home of Eleanor's sporting element. The Telluride was halfway up the first block beside an alley. As they approached this alley, a voice shouted, "Sheriff Moses?"

"John?" Moses recognized John Lieninger's voice.

"Keep your hands away from your gunbelts." Lieninger stepped into the street aiming a twelve gauge side-by-side at Moses' and Mudeater's heads. "You know these scatter-guns have a wide spread, so both of you be smart and don't do anything except stand still." Musgrove trailed Lieninger out of the alley. Duggan followed Musgrove. Lieninger whistled and two dozen masked men emerged from the surrounding shadows like wraiths from a bone orchard fog. All brought rifles. One carried a rope under one arm.

"You might want to reconsider this, John."

"Keep quiet, Jeb, until we attend to this Sioux."

Mudeater, who had slitted his eyes and appeared to be sleeping on his feet, perked to life. "Where's a Sioux?"

One masked man cocked his rifle and leveled it at Mudeater's left ear. "Maybe you ain't one of the cross killers, but no Sioux belongs south of Wyoming. Not after the battle of the Greasy Grass. Some of us had kin with Custer and the Seventh."

"I'm sorry, but the truth is I'm not Sioux. Even if I was Sioux, I'd only be half Sioux because I'm half white, which doesn't matter because I'm half Cherokee."

"Shut up!" The masked man jammed his rifle's barrel against Mudeater's ear, cutting the lobe. *"String him up!"*

Inside the Telluride, people heard the masked man's shout followed by a ruckus of cheers. Kirk, nursing a beer at the bar, immediately guessed what was going on. Snatching his Henry from the rack beside the door, he bolted outside.

Kirk charged the vigilantes from behind, aiming the Henry. "Throw 'em up!"

When the vigilantes turned Kirk's way, Moses took aim at Lieninger's crew while Mudeater buffaloed the man who cut his ear.

Kirk asked, "What do you want to do with them, Sheriff?"

The vigilantes were flummoxed. They outnumbered their opponents nearly nine-to-one, but had never counted on getting into a fire-fight with three blooded gunmen.

"John? Tell your boys to pile their firearms there in the middle of the street. Hop to it."

Lieninger gave the order as one man raised his rifle in Mudeater and Moses' direction.

Kirk fired and yelled, "Look out!"

The bullet pierced the diehard's left forearm and he dropped his rifle.

Moses, Mudeater, and Kirk corralled the vigilantes and herded the lot down Riffle Street. Coleman, lugging his Peacemakers and breathing hard, met the parade as it rounded Argos. He could not believe what he saw any more than the crowd could gathering along the sidewalks. "What happened?"

"Just a little misunderstanding," Mudeater commented with a wink.

"I'll tell it to you later," Moses promised. "Run back to the jail and get the cells open. Scrounge up more blankets if we need them. Company's coming."

CHAPTER TWELVE

"I want to come home, Ella. Let me come home, Ella."

The woman wearing slave clothes stopped rocking to pat the boy's head. "Stop talkin' silliness, chil'." She looked down at him, revealing a face which looked like Ella's. "You is home. Home to stay."

Ella Brand jerked awake and almost screamed. First from fear, then frustration. She had enough of her nightmare and did not appreciate this latest permutation.

Daybreak was threatening. In spite of the early hour, Ella heard voices down in the study. Joshua and Jeb were talking and neither sounded sociable.

No one in this house can seem to be happy anymore.

Pulling back the bedclothes, she moved to the window to watch the sunrise. At least she could still enjoy that. Then, just like on the morning her brother returned, Ella glimpsed candlelight pass behind the planks of the playroom window next door.

"Someone *is* in there!" Slipping on a robe, she scuttled to the study. "There's an intruder next door!"

"In your barn?" Moses asked.

Joshua knew different. "No. The Kirk house. Ella thought she saw a light in one of its windows a few nights ago."

"Who could be over there?"

Neither Brand suggested an answer.

"Want me to look?"

"Yes!" Ella yelped, but her husband, staring out at the debilitated mansion, said, "No. I don't see anything."

Ella started to protest, "But Josh!"

"What?" Joshua yanked a pistol out of a desk drawer and tossed it to his wife, who caught it in spite of her astonishment. "Here! Go see for yourself if some boogey is haunting your old house!"

She gawked, dumbfounded.

Moses felt a need to say something. "Look, it's no problem for me to—"

"*Your* problem," Joshua insisted, "is the twenty-seven men you have incarcerated."

"Jeb?" asked Ella, and Moses explained. "So Paul is running with a half-breed Indian now. What must people in Denver or back east think if they know?"

Joshua laughed with bitter amusement. "I swear, Ella, sometimes listening to you, it's like father never died! If you aren't fretting about what folks you consider proper are thinking, you're thinking the worst of the improper ones. This 'half-breed' is a Pinkerton and a government scout. He's a man risking his life searching for the cross killers."

Moses added, "For what it's worth, Mudeater seems like a good duck, Ella."

Joshua asked Moses, "What do you intend to do with the men you arrested?"

"I'll spring 'em soon as I get back. They've learned their lesson. Even if they haven't, I doubt any of them will want to lock horns with Kirk and Mudeater again. I just wanted to tell you what was what before they came here to chew your ear."

"Fine. Thank you."

Moses again asked Ella if she wanted him to check on the light she had seen. She obviously did, but instead politely declined the offer. "No, Jeb. I'm sure Joshua's right. It was nothing."

"Fine, then." Moses made his farewell.

Ella stared at the Persian carpet. When she did not say anything, Joshua took up the pistol. "I'm sorry I lost my temper, said the things I did. It wasn't the time for it. I'll go over and have a look for you."

Ella had every intention of letting him until she remembered: "*Stop talkin' silliness, chil'. You is home. Home to stay.*"

"Please, don't."

"Why not?"

"I had a nightmare. I've been upset. I'm sure you're right. I was imagining."

"I don't mind making sure."

"I do," she said, her timbre harsh. Then, softening, "I'm scared of what you might find over there."

"What do you mean?"

"I don't know, and I don't want to know. That house holds nothing but painful memories. I don't want you stirring them up."

"You talk like the place is haunted!"

"I just think it's better if we leave it alone. Please, do what I ask. After what you've done and said, you owe me that much."

"You're right. I do." He laid the pistol back on the desk.

"Thank you." She did not leave. Ella wanted to, but she could not budge. The part of her nearest Joshua would not obey. Unable to stop herself, she said, "We should get away. We need to get away. To mourn and forget some of our hurt if we can."

A flicker of hope tickled his heart. "Really? Do you mean that?"

"You said a while ago that you should be involved with deciding which railroad wins the right of way into Leadville."

"That was before Jon."

"The business still needs doing, and nothing is preventing us from turning it to our personal advantage." She touched his face, eyes blurry under tears. "We don't stand a chance if we stay here."

"I'll have to spend a couple of days at the Leadville office first, but I could meet you in Denver."

"As long as we're away from here."

That was all Joshua needed to hear. "I'll go into town this morning and begin making arrangements. With luck I can leave early next week." He reached to touch her face, but she retreated a step, avoiding his fingertips.

"Not yet. Please."

"Of course." Feeling doltish, he tried not to sound hurt.

She walked to the door. "Joshua?"

Hearing her say his name again was a tonic. "Yes?"

"If I said I loved you, would you believe me?"

"Without doubt."

"Good." She made herself leave before he saw her smile.

Moses, a man of his word, released his prisoners as soon as he came down from the bluff. "I'll keep your firearms. Call it your fine and consider yourselves lucky. Now get before I come to my senses."

The vigilantes did not have to be told twice.

Coleman asked, "Do you think this is a good idea?"

"It's a better one than trying to keep them locked up. Not that Josh would have put up with it if I tried."

"You're the law. Not Mr. Brand."

"True. Problem is, none of those yahoos got the chance to do much law-breaking. So what do you suggest I do?"

The deputy had no suggestions.

"Did Mudeater go back to the tableland like he said?"

"Right after you went up the bluff."

"And Kirk's at the Occidental?"

"As far as I know."

"Uh-huh." Moses started shutting cell doors. "Young man, are you up to some traveling?"

"Where to?"

Moses closed the last door. "How well did you know Travis Morgan back when he was sheriff here?"

"As well as any kid did then, I guess."

"Morgan quit right after Amos Kirk was hung, didn't he?"

"You know he did, Mose. Well, soon after, anyway."

"I heard Morgan moved to Denver and enlisted with Cook."

Coleman said he had heard the same.

"All right, I want you to ride to Lake City. Pick up the stage to Pueblo then get on the next train west. With any luck you can be in Denver this time tomorrow."

"Denver? You want me to find Sheriff Morgan?"

"You catch on fast."

"What do I do if I find him?"

Moses actually smiled. "One thing I learned about Morgan way back when he was chasing me, the law comes first with him. He lives and he'll die by it. You tell him everything that's happened since Paul Kirk got here. Then tell him that the law in Eleanor needs to know anything he might know about the Brands and the Kirks. Especially Amos Kirk killing Luther Brand."

"Why ask him about that?"

Moses remembered Ella's warning about Kirk, and what Kirk had said at the Telluride about family. He also remembered Kirk saying, " 'The

Brands and I have a history,' " and wondered if there was more to that history than just family.

"I'm playing a hunch, Teddy. That's all I've got. But that hunch tells me I'd best find out all I can about the Brands and Kirks before something worth thwarting happens."

CHAPTER THIRTEEN

Ella kept to the bedroom until Joshua left for town. Watching him ride the App out of the barn, she waited for him to reach the bottom of the bluff, then hurried downstairs to grab the pistol from the study.

Crossing to the neighboring house, Ella forced down her eyes. She had no desire to see where she was traveling, and even after fifteen years she could make this journey blindfolded. *The heart never forgets*, she thought to herself, as much as she would have preferred otherwise.

On the veranda she inspected the boards barricading the front door. Sure enough, the nails were snug but not tight. Someone had been carefully removing the boards then replacing them.

"Someone," she spat.

Standing these boards beside the door, Ella Brand entered her childhood home.

Ella had forgotten she had had the furniture,

busts, and paintings covered, and Amos' collection
of law books packed away. Why she had bothered,
she could not recall. The polished wood and brass
were filthy and tarnished, and dust had grown
thick enough on cobwebs to snap several of their
sticky strands, giving them the look of gray tat-
tered rags hung to dry. Field mice had taken up
residence in the walls, judging by the skitterings
she heard and the stink of droppings polluting the
air, and no doubt the garret where she and Paul
and Joshua had played pirates as children was
now a roost for hermit thrush and camp-robbers.

Walking upstairs, hugging the banister to avoid
the peeling linen-covered walls, she found scuffs in
the dust carpeting the second-story hall. A man
who was light on his feet had walked here many
times the past few days. Ahead, the playroom door
stood open.

"Paul?" She cocked the pistol. "Are you here?"

She peaked inside and saw the light blue linen
walls, parquet floor, and all of the furniture covered with sheets. All except Lara Kirk's rocking
chair. It sat exposed in the corner by the window.
Someone had spread a horse blanket beside the
rocker and was using an old saddle bag for a pil-
low. Spying something she sensed was familiar on
the rocker's seat, Ella crept over to see what it was.

"A Bible?" The Kirks' family Bible. "I thought
we'd lost that." She reached for it.

"Hello."

Ella swung the pistol around, and Paul grabbed
its barrel and twisted the grip out of her hand.

"Where . . . ? How did you . . . ?"

"I've learned to sleep lightly and tread nimbly."

She backed away a step. "From your Indian friend, no doubt."

"No doubt. How are you?"

"I thought you were staying at the Occidental."

"In my work, it pays not to sleep where people think you do."

"How long have you been staying here?"

"Since the morning I came to town."

"I should have known." Ella looked at the saddle bag and blanket. "Why in here?"

"I like the memories."

Ella shook her head. "That's silly."

"Why are you here?"

"Because I saw your candlelight."

"When?" He asked as if he already knew the answer.

"The morning you came to town, then again before sunrise today."

"It took you almost a week to build up the nerve to come over here? You used to be made of sterner stuff."

"It took me almost a week to decide it was worth the trouble. I typically don't care what happens to this place or anyone foolish enough to be in it."

"So it appears." He picked up the Bible. "Well, this room does hold good memories for me. Heaven knows I haven't collected very many since we abandoned it for the outside world."

"You didn't come back to Eleanor after fourteen years to haunt our playroom."

Paul sat in the rocker and put the Bible and pistol in his lap. "I thought that would have been obvious after our talk outside the jailhouse the other day. I came back to find your son's killers."

"Why? You didn't even know him."

"What does that matter? He's blood. My nephew. Maybe the closest thing I'll ever have to a son."

"Spare me your life story—I'm not interested."

"The devil you aren't. So long as you and I share the same mother, you'll always be interested in my life story."

Ella shook her head again.

Paul said, "You and Josh dug your own graves the day they buried Papa beside Mama. I can't say I appreciate some of the decisions you two made then and since, but I don't begrudge them. If I did, you'd have been a widow long ago, and you know it."

Ella's body rattled.

"Jon, however, had his whole life in front of him. People tell me he exhibited the best of the Kirks and the Brands. You can delude yourself if you must, Ella, but those are pretty good bloodlines to sire a colt." He held out Ella's pistol.

"I don't want to hear this!" Snatching her pistol, she stomped towards the door. "If you really came back because of Jon, shouldn't you stop playing ring-a-ring-a-rosies with your precious memories and do your job? Find who killed my child!"

"I have."

She quickly looked his way.

"I said, 'I have,'" he repeated. "To my satisfaction, anyway. I've deduced their hideout's general location and when they'll likely try to strike again. I'm not going into details, but, if I'm right, this will be over soon."

"Have you told Jeb?"

"It's too soon. I really shouldn't have told you yet."

"Tell him!" she begged. "Quit beating around the stump and go bring these murderers to justice! Give Joshua and me some peace! Please!"

"It's too risky. Their hideout is so isolated any search now will scare them off. Maybe to a new lair. Maybe for good."

"Waiting puts innocent lives at risk."

"Going after them now could put even more lives at risk. I can't do that."

Ella knew better than to try and change her brother's mind. There were times when Paul, like their father, was so sure he knew best. "If innocent blood is spilled, pray that Heaven takes pity on you, because no one in this town will."

"If it can't be helped, I'll take what comes. You've always worried too much about what people think, Ella."

"And you never cared enough!"

"I care about you. That's all that should really matter. Family is all that really matters when you come right down to it."

Ella scrunched her eyebrows, kinking them into an angry bow. "You sound like Amos."

"Paw would do anything for his family. Sacrifice anything. You can't deny that."

"You can think what you will of me, but I have no delusions so far as it comes to what Amos would do when it came to family."

"Ella, I can't blame you for being angry—"

"I'm not angry. I've been nothing but *furious* for fourteen years! Amos went way past the line!"

"What line?"

"The line between his family and mine. Between the Kirks and Joshua, Jon, and I."

"I still don't . . ."

"I was married, Paul! I had a son! You and Amos weren't my family any longer. Josh and Jon were."

"That's nonsense! Having a husband and child doesn't change the fact that you're Amos Kirk's daughter! It doesn't change that you and I are blood!"

"Maybe you should open our Bible and read what it has to say about that: 'A man shall leave his father and mother and be joined to his wife, and the two shall become one flesh.'"

"And maybe you should read the fifth commandment. Look, Ella, I'll never deny that Paw carried matters too far. But he had his reasons, and he loved you and Jon."

"I know." She said this like she meant it. "There was a time Amos loved Josh too. Like a son."

"Until we went behind his back."

"Yes. *We.* You knew how our father felt, but still you helped Josh and me to elope. You stood up for Josh! But Amos only wanted to blame my husband for what *we* did."

It was Paul's turn to shake his head. "Paw wasn't too happy with you or me either."

"But he blamed Josh! Amos wanted to take me away from Josh! From my husband and the father of my son! Amos may not have been at our wedding to give me away, but that doesn't mean I didn't leave his family to make one of my own with Josh!" She pointed at the Bible in Paul's lap, and, eyes brightening from the threat of tears, said, "Amos should have respected that."

"You're right. I said I'd never deny he carried things too far. In the heat of the moment, our father let you down. And he hurt you. But he's dead, Ella. Can't you forgive him? How can you and I ever be a family again until you do?"

Ella stared at Paul. "Could you forgive Amos?"

"Yes. I've forgiven Josh, haven't I?"

She blinked, bit her lower lip, and tried as hard as she could not to surrender to the part of her that agreed with Paul. Shutting it out, she informed her brother, "I don't believe you have forgiven Joshua. I truly don't believe you ever will."

"How can you say that?" He stood up, insulted, his fingers digging into the Bible's cover.

"I can because you and I are blood, Paul, and I know I will never forgive Amos. So how can I believe you could forgive Joshua?" She turned to leave. "I can't and I won't."

Paul watched her desert the playroom then listened to her footsteps as she got out of their house. Going to the window, he peered through the planks and watched his only living family march as fast as she could to the other Victorian. He was still looking long after she disappeared inside the pristine Brand House. He would have given anything—even his soul—to be with her.

For the first time since that horrible day at Murfreesboro Paul Kirk felt like crying.

CHAPTER FOURTEEN

On a regular day, with the sun dipping low in the sky, the Fairchilds would have made camp and started supper. Today they pushed on. With pemmican to sustain them, they reckoned to reach Eleanor soon after nightfall.

Bartholomew was driving the lead wagon with their house packed in back, passing time by reciting verse to his family and any horse that cared to listen: "Gaily bedight, A gallant knight, In sunshine and in shadow, Had journeyed long, Singing a song, In search of Eldorado."

Kathryn followed while Penny, who had spent most of the day driving the second wagon, was curled up in the rear with her parents' other possessions trying to nap.

"'And, as his strength Failed him at length, He met a pilgrim shadow,'" Bartholomew continued. "'Shadow,' said he, 'Where can it be—This land of Eldorado?'"

There was not a cloud in the gloaming as Penny listened to her father and started to drowse.

" 'Over the Mountains of the Moon, Down the valley of the Shadow, ride, boldly ride,' the shade replied, 'If you seek for . . .' "

Her father stopped the same moment Penny thought she heard the crack of thunder. Such a thing was not impossible, especially in the mountains, but it was peculiar.

Bartholomew's ears, acclimated to the cacophony of war, knew the noise was not the sound of thunder, but before he could shout a warning there came another crack.

CHAPTER FIFTEEN

The moon, as lean as a scythe, was peaking over the San Juans as Mudeater barreled into Eleanor, whipping the reins of the Fairchilds' second wagon with Penny propped against him. Shouting at the people in the streets to "Get outta my way!" Mudeater raced on until he reached Doc Gluzunov's westside office on Tannenbaum Street. Jumping from the wagon, he rushed around the agitated bystanders and frothing horses to take hold of Penny.

"Doc! Doc! Get out here!" He scooped Penny down off the wagon as Gluzunov waddled out of the office. "Help her, Doc."

Gluzunov observed that the young woman's skin was pale, cool, and moist. Her pulse was rapid and weak, and her breathing was shallow. Oblivious to the excitement around her, the woman's eyes were dull with dilated pupils.

"She get sick? Been trembling?"

"No, Doc. She tried speaking to me after I found her, but had trouble talking. Then she stopped trying and got like this."

"I think shock. Will know better when we take her inside. What happen to her?"

"The bushwhackers . . ." Mudeater began explaining as Gluzunov shut the office door. That ignited the crowd to chattering, which combusted into a conflagration a few seconds later when a dead Apache was spotted stuffed into the back of the wagon.

Two minutes after that Moses stepped into Gluzunov's office. He found Mudeater alone in the waiting room.

"Where is she?"

Mudeater jerked a thumb towards Gluzunov's consulting room. "Doc said to tell you to wait out here with me."

Respecting Gluzunov's orders, Moses grabbed a chair.

"You want to tell me about that Apache outside?"

"Him and three Mexicans shot two people in the head that young lady I brought in was traveling with. They were going to kill her, too, until I showed up."

Gluzunov's front door opened again. Kirk entered, Ned Scott dogging his heels. The journalist, observing the half-breed, held out his hand. "You must be Mudeater. I'm sorry I missed meeting you last night. That sounded like some excitement, though it appears you've topped that. Is that Apache a cross killer?"

Mudeater shook Scott's hand and repeated what he told Moses.

Scott wondered aloud why an Apache was running with Mexicans in Colorado.

"The Apache's a mercenary. Didn't you see the way he's dressed?" Kirk grumbled. With Ella's admonition about innocent lives ringing in his ears, he asked his partner, "What about the Mexicans? Get a good look at them? See where they headed after you chased them away?"

"I never got near enough for a good look. They split off every which way but south. One was big enough to hunt bears with a switch, I can tell you that much."

Moses straightened up. "A real big Mexican, you say?"

"He blocked a lot of sun. Abe Lincoln might have got himself a crick looking up at this *grande hombre*."

"Could he have been carrying an 1859 Sharps? The kind with a double-set trigger?"

"Don't know. I don't think he had a carbine or short rifle. Why?"

"Back in my outlaw days I was acquainted with a Mexican road-agent named Pedro Hernandez. Huge fellow. A giant. Mighty fine marksman, too, and he's got a pair of brothers who are just as deadly."

Scott inquired if Hernandez was still an outlaw.

"Not exactly. Back when Colorado and New Mexico were wrangling about statehood, Pedro went and got himself chosen as a Mexican delegate to the joint-legislature in Denver. The story goes that some dunderheaded Colorado delegates got to calling him 'Big Foot.' Pedro always claimed to be descended from the right honorable General

Don Pedro de Villasur, so maybe that's why, instead of killing those idiots on the spot, he challenged them to a duel."

"How many dunderheads were there?"

"Seven. And Pedro didn't care if he killed them one at a time or all at once. About then those Coloradoans requested that the law escort him out of Denver. Pedro left peaceably and went home to New Mexico, where last I heard he's become a regular patriot."

Mudeater exchanged knowing stares with Kirk. "Hernandez sounds like the sort of man you've been looking for, old son."

Kirk shrugged.

Moses asked, "You two know something you ought to be telling me?"

Kirk looked like he could start cussing again as he perched on a chair beside the consulting room door. "I'll tell you after the doctor lets us know if the lady will be all right."

Scott started to press but Moses, who had learned his lesson when it came to Kirk, cut him off. "Not now."

The sheriff and manhunter traded scowls as they waited for Gluzunov.

Chapter Sixteen

Coleman's first stop upon reaching Denver the following morning was the police station. Establishing his credentials, he inquired about his town's former sheriff.

"Morgan?" an officer at the front desk laughed. "That old bronco? I reckon he's home having supper."

"It's only nine."

"He only went home an hour ago, deputy."

"Could you tell me how to find his house?"

Another officer, a handsome young gent named Axel Peterson, offered to take Coleman there. Grateful at first, Coleman soon felt self-conscious walking alongside Peterson through the capital. The deputy was dusty from his journey and scraggily after not shaving for two mornings, while the policeman was spotlessly attired in uniform and snappy hat. Peterson pointed out various shops and homes of interest as well as an amusement park along their way. As for Morgan, Peterson confided, "I hope to be half the man he is twenty years hence. If Dave Cook is the Aramis of Denver lawmen, Morgan's the D'Artagnan."

"I had no idea." Coleman had no idea what Peterson was talking about. "We haven't heard much about the sheriff since he left the San Juans after the war."

"He tired of the mountains, eh?"

"No. He was good friends with the town's founders, Luther Brand and Amos Kirk. Then one day Mr. Kirk shot Mr. Brand during some sort of argument, leaving Morgan to oversee Kirk's hanging. I was only thirteen at the time, but even a kid like me could see Morgan couldn't stand living in Eleanor after that."

Peterson grunted. "He never discusses his days as a sheriff. That must be why."

"Nice to hear he's gotten his legs under him again."

"That he has. Just last week he arrested eight hoboes."

Coleman, who had watched Morgan tame rowdy gangs of cowhands with only a revolver and shotgun, said, "Oh."

"Listen to this: Morgan was told about a nest of thieves hiding in the cellar of a vacant building along Blake Street, near Sixteenth. When he got there he found straw laying everywhere, two feet deep in spots, so he rummaged around and kept rummaging until he found seven men and one woman."

"You did say eight."

"They were what we call 'California hoboes.' A

seedy lot. Fighters too. Morgan needed five minutes to subdue them and line them up into twos."

"Why fight? Why didn't he draw on them?"

"No artillery. Morgan had been taking a walk on his day off at the time, and he didn't bother to retrieve his revolver from home before heading to the cellar."

Now Coleman was impressed.

"Morgan marched the gang to a patrol box at Fifteenth and Blake. Things seemed well in hand until he pulled for the wagon. The hoboes got skittish and jumped him again. Morgan laid out four of them, but by then he was wearing down, and he says things looked mighty blue for him until a Negro helped subdue the others."

"Good man!" Coleman couldn't help cheering the Samaritan.

"I'd be proud to shake his hand. After the wagon hauled away the hoboes, Morgan returned to the cellar and found any amount of stolen articles, including a nearly full keg of beer. Who wouldn't want to be like that man at his age?"

With each passing block Coleman found himself liking Denver. He liked the city even more after they reached Morgan's house, Peterson knocked on the front door, and it was opened by a petite young woman in her early twenties with amethyst eyes, milky skin, and hair as black as a velvet ribbon.

"Afternoon, Miss Morgan. This gentleman is Deputy Ted Coleman of Eleanor, Colorado. He has come to see Detective Morgan on urgent business."

"Won't you come in?" She escorted the men into the sitting room. "Can I offer you some lemonade?" Both visitors said that would be fine, and she left to tell Morgan he had guests.

"Who was that?" Coleman asked, praying he did not sound like an over-anxious hayseed.

"That's his daughter. I suppose she would have been in pigtails last you saw her. Imagine she's changed some since then."

Coleman was going to tell Peterson that the woman could not be Morgan's daughter, but she returned then with Morgan. Eleanor's old sheriff did not seem to recognize Coleman from Jacob at first, but then exclaimed, "It is! Teddy Coleman! All grown! And Moses made you of all people his deputy!"

All Al Long wanted was some lunch.

Roused from sound slumber three hours before dawn, the collier had been working nonstop since, making emergency repairs on the roof of one of the Riffle Street smelters' charcoal kilns. Smeared black like a coal miner, Long was frazzled and famished as he trudged to his trim frame house, the last home on the left on Powderhorn Street. Or it was when he left before cockcrow.

Someone was erecting a prefabricated house in the adjoining vacant lot.

"Hey! *Hey!*"

Long chased the *pound-pound-pound*ing of hammering to a ladder, where Paul Kirk was putting the finishing touches on the north wall.

Up on the bluff, Joshua stood watching from a window in his study. He had been there for hours, ever since Kirk and Mudeater returned with the Fairchilds' bodies and second wagon. Joshua found himself sympathizing with Long's obvious indignation as Juanita brought Brand some coffee. He thanked the housemaid, sipped, and waited to see what the men below did.

Kirk bid Long, "Good afternoon."

"You can't put this here! This lot belongs to the Nox!"

"I'm aware of that." Kirk hammered.

"This isn't your land!"

Without missing a beat with the hammer: "Do you know who I am?"

"Of course I do. Who doesn't?"

"Then you must know that I own this land and can do whatever I want with it."

"What are you talking about? The Kirks forfeited their share of the Nox the day your father murdered Luther Brand."

"Not true."

"It is!"

The only reply was resumed hammering.

"Knock it off! I don't want you here! You have no right to be here!"

Something that Long mistook for a bird swooped from the ladder and *thudd*ed between his boots. He peeked down, saw a screwdriver handle sticking in the earth between his toes, looked back up, and shrieked to see Kirk standing one step away from his face, hammer drawn back like a savage readying to bury a tomahawk.

Joshua dropped his coffee cup. "Paul! No!"

The collier was convinced this was his dead man's moment, but Kirk just dared him to go fetch the sheriff. "Fetch Joshua, too, if you want," he added. "And you can tell them if anyone lays a hand on this house except the lady who owns it, I will leave this town. Today." Lowering the hammer, Kirk went back to work.

"Dora May, fetch that lemonade like a good girl. Axel, give her a hand."

They did as requested as Morgan closed the sitting room's door.

"Rest your bones, Teddy."

Coleman, more self-conscious than before, hesitated.

"I said sit."

He sat. "It's good to see you again, Sheriff."

" 'Sheriff'? That's 'detective' now, though there are days I think the title is the only difference between the jobs." Morgan had gained a few pounds and his yellow hair was thinner on top, but those appeared to be the man's only concessions to age. Gangly and strong as a moose, with a face wrinkled from experience, too much sun and too many hard trails, Morgan was striking but not pretty.

"Did Officer Peterson introduce you to my daughter?"

Coleman nodded.

"You were probably too young to remember her back in Ella?" Mischief twinkled in Morgan's pale purple eyes.

"Yes, sir, I must have been too young."

A deafening laugh. "Sam sure taught you manners, Teddy! Your pappy would be proud of you!"

"Thank you, sir."

"I married Dora May's mother in '66, after I was sure I was staying in Denver."

Coleman nodded once more.

"I adopted Dora May that same year. She was eight at the time. Her father was killed at Gettysburg."

Coleman relaxed. "I'm sorry to hear that."

"So am I. Her father, Curtis Morgan, was my elder brother."

"Again, my sympathies, sir." He brushed some rude black strands away from in front of his eyes. "I don't think anyone in Eleanor knew about your brother at the time."

"Amos and Luther, that's all. I only mention that because you came all this way to ask me about them."

"Sheriff Moses wired you I was coming?"

More laughing. "Can you believe that? Jeb Moses? Sheriff! I'd never have thought it! I bet he's a good one. Old outlaws do seem to make the best lawmen. They have more to amend, I suppose." Morgan walked to a table where he picked up a copy of the *Denver Times* and delivered it to Coleman. "No, Moses didn't wire me. I read between the lines of this article."

It was news about the latest cross killing, telegraphed to the *Times* by Ned Scott. The article mentioned Paul Kirk and Mudeater as Pinkerton agents brought in to assist Sheriff Jeb Moses in the pursuit of the cross killers.

"Twenty-nine dead now." Coleman crumpled the edges of the paper without realizing.

Morgan liked seeing such anger in a lawman. "So Amos' boy is home again."

"Yes, sir. Joshua Brand hired Mr. Kirk after his son was killed last month."

"I read about Jon. At the time I was half-tempted

to offer my help to Moses, but I figured he wouldn't appreciate it. I wouldn't have, any more than I'd of appreciated Josh hiring Paul."

"That's the reason I'm here, sir. Mr. Brand hired Mr. Kirk, but he wants nothing personally to do with the man. His wife is Kirk's sister, Ella, who warned the sheriff that her brother could be as dangerous as his father."

Morgan decided it was time to rest his feet. "Amos Kirk was a lot of things, but dangerous was not one of them. He could be an odd stick, but so could Luther. Tell me, have you met Paul? What's your opinion of him?"

"He's polite. Friendly, but not outgoing. In that and other ways he reminds me of Mr. Brand."

"Oh? What other ways?"

"They both seem so smart. Like Judge Berthel, I mean. Educated men."

"I can tell you that they *are* smart. So's Ella. Their pappies saw to that themselves. Did you know Amos and Luther were professors before they became sourdoughs?"

"I don't think I did, sir."

"Taught at Patrick Henry in Richmond."

"Then I guess their children would be quick at their books, though none of them are lilies. All three would fight a rattler and give him first bite. Mr. Kirk in particular would have trouble finding a fight with intelligent men."

Morgan nodded. "His reputation puts him among the first rank of manhunters."

"Sir, Sheriff Moses is worried that there's some sort of dark secret between the Brands and Kirk. If you don't mind, would you tell him . . . I mean me . . . whatever you might know about their families, in particular about Amos Kirk killing Luther Brand?"

Morgan arched his eyebrows. "I may not have always seen eye-to-eye with Amos or Luther on some things, but they were my good friends. If I knew anything about them by way of a confidence, why would I betray it to you and Moses?"

"If you were still Eleanor's sheriff, would you want to know if there was any reason to be concerned about the Brands and Kirks? Especially with the concerns Mrs. Brand has expressed about her own brother?"

Morgan was getting to like Coleman more each minute. "You're game, Teddy. Moses can be proud of you too. Yes, you're right, I would want to know." He shouted in the direction of the kitchen, "Time for lemonade!" then faced Coleman. "And dinner. I wager you haven't eaten since leaving Eleanor."

Lake City was more accurate, but still, his priorities were about gathering information. "Sir?" he said.

"Patience, Teddy. You've broached a delicate matter. Give an old man time to think."

Peterson entered with their glasses on a tray and Dora May followed with a sweating pitcher of lemonade. Coleman was as parched as he was hungry, but all he could look at was Dora May, who did not seem to mind the deputy's stare.

Morgan, blessed with excellent vision, mumbled, "And you're giving me a lot to think about."

CHAPTER SEVENTEEN

Long forgot about lunch. He galloped to the sheriff's office, where Moses glumly studied a territorial chart rolled out across one of the desks.

"Sheriff, that rep Kirk is putting up a prefab next to my house!"

"Uh-huh."

"What are you going to do about it?"

"Am I supposed to do something?" Moses opened a desk drawer and scrounged without looking until his hand found a magnifying glass.

"You know that land belongs to the Nox! I told Kirk he can't use it without permission!"

Concentrating on the chart through the glass, Moses suggested Kirk might have asked permission.

"Mr. Brand would never give it to him! Besides, Kirk tried to kill me!"

"Oh, Al!" Moses dropped the glass on the chart.

"Paul Kirk doesn't 'try' to kill anyone. 'Sides, why would he want to plant you in Boot Hill?"

"All I know is he threw a screwdriver between my boots then reared a hammer at me!"

"Yet here you are. So what happened? You kill Kirk in self-defense? If you did, your problem's solved."

"Now, Sheriff!!"

"Al, that prefab belongs to the woman Kirk's partner rescued. Kirk's probably putting it up in case the poor thing wants to stay in Eleanor after she collects her wits. And he just probably wanted to scare you off so he could work in peace."

"Oh." Long blushed.

"Kirk and his partner spent all last night searching for the cross killers, and came back empty-handed a couple of hours ago. That must be when he started putting up that prefab."

"No need to ladle it on. I'm sorry."

"Good." Moses returned to the chart.

"I reckon I can't blame him for getting sore like he did. Now that I think about it, he must have thought I knew that was her house."

"Is that so?" Moses wondered if he had a screwdriver or hammer lying around handy himself.

"He said he didn't care if I fetched you or Mr. Brand, but that he'd leave town if anyone except the lady who owned that house laid a hand on it. I was so scared, the fact he mentioned a lady flew past by me."

"He said he'd leave town? That's sort of a queer threat."

Or maybe not.

The night before, after Gluzunov informed the

men in his waiting room that the young woman would be fine after some rest, Kirk explained that he had a general idea where to find the bushwhackers' hideout and when the ambushers would strike next. "Or, I thought I knew when." Kirk explained his theory regarding August 1. Scott was skeptical, but Moses said, "You know, if Pedro is part of this, that makes sense."

"Come on, Sheriff!"

"No, Ned, now listen. When Colorado became a territory back in '61, a big knob of land belonging to the territory of New Mexico got cut off at the 37th parallel. A lot of New Mexicans lost a lot of land, including the demesnes of Sangre de Cristo, Nolan, Baca, and Maxwell."

"I'm sure it was tragic for them, but what has that to do with Statehood Day?"

"As long as Colorado was still a territory, those New Mexicans who lost their land in '61 had a chance of getting it back. But statehood made Colorado's borders permanent. What if these ambushes are the killers' way of exacting retribution on Coloradoans for what they see as claim-jumping?"

Mudeater asked, "Where did you say this knob was?"

"Pretty much everything south and west of Eleanor. And pretty much everything north up to the Ute reservation and east of the Great Divide. That's why so many places in these parts have Spanish names."

"Which," Kirk cut in, "could explain why the bushwhackings have not only been committed in Colorado, but in this specific vicinity."

Scott slapped his forehead. "Why didn't we notice this coincidence before? Then there is no sig-nificance to Eleanor being in the hub of the cross killings?"

"I think Eleanor isn't so much in a hub as sort of on the other side of the Divide from White Park."

Scott knew the spot. "What does White Park have to do with this?"

"That's where I believe the bushwhackers have their hideout."

Moses had to disagree. "We searched White Park. Me, Teddy, and a couple of dozen other men. We didn't see so much as a bent blade of grass."

"Those other men who searched White Park with you and your deputy? Were they scouts and trackers?"

"Yes. Some of the best in the territory."

"Did you thoroughly search White Park?"

"Of course we did!"

"Okay. Do you have a chart of the territory we're discussing?"

"Sure. In my office."

"Let's go take a look at it." Before heading to the jailhouse, Kirk said to Gluzunov, "Please have the young lady moved to my room at the Occidental when you think she is up to it. It's hers for as long as she requires. I'll see to her bills at the hotel, with you, and anywhere else while she remains in Eleanor." His tone left no doubt that these were in-structions, not requests.

At the jailhouse Moses unrolled the chart Long had found him scrutinizing. "There you go, Mr. Kirk."

"Thank you." But Kirk was curious about some-thing else. "Where's Deputy Coleman?"

"Out doing his job."

Kirk pretended to forget about the matter. "Okay. According to my research, Sheriff, you, the absent Deputy Coleman, and some of the best scouts and trackers in the territory have searched this area," he drew an invisible loop around southwest Colorado with his index finger, "for three years, supposedly with a thoroughness that would put a geological survey to shame."

Scott remarked, "You like that word. 'Thorough.' "

"Not as much as I'd like to know how four men can evade such a dedicated manhunt for that length of time, Ned."

"That Apache might explain some of it," Mudeater suggested. "Bandidos couldn't escape that big a posse for three years, but an Apache is a different story."

"It's still unlikely," Kirk riposted. "In my opinion, it's impossible."

Moses philosophized that it was not impossible if it was true.

Scott asked, "How do you know the bush-whackers' hideout isn't outside the San Juans? Maybe even Colorado? If this Hernandez is responsible for the cross killings, it would make more sense for him to hole up in the New Mexico territory than our state."

"If you document where and when the ambushes transpired on a chart like this one, you will see that the vast majority have taken place within an asymmetrical hundred-mile circumference that includes Eleanor. None north of it, and very few south besides the last ambushes of '76, '77, and '78. Those three, interestingly, all happened in October within the respective proximities of Cortez, Durango, and Pagosa Springs."

"They were heading back to the New Mexico territory before winter," Moses realized. "Why didn't I see that?"

"What matters is that we've discovered this in time to prevent them from escaping south this season."

Mudeater agreed. "If Hernandez is part of this, and if he is a patriot, we'd never find him and his men in New Mexico. Even if we could, we'd never make it back to Colorado with them alive."

"I'd have to try," Moses told them. "All right, let's say I go along with you that our boys are holed up somewhere in this big ring. Why do you think it's White Park?"

Kirk said, "The only way the bushwhackers can have avoided capture this long is if their hideout is somewhere you haven't searched; but, you claim to have searched the Gunnison country, the San Luis Valley, the Rio Grande Valley . . ."

"Everywhere," Moses interjected. "We've searched everywhere there is to search in and around the San Juans. Including White Park."

"Thoroughly?"

"There's that word again," Scott remarked.

"Look, we can agree that their hideout is within this circumference. Logic therefore suggests that it must be somewhere too wild or isolated to permit a meticulous search—and White Park fits the bill."

"Wild and isolated describes a lot of the parks within your circumference."

"That's not entirely true, Ned. Every other park in this vicinity is at least used by ranchers to feed their stock during the summer months, but even prospectors avoid White Park because it is too remote and primitive. Sheriff Moses, can you honestly tell me that you, your deputy, and some of the finest scouts and trackers in Colorado were able to search every canyon, ravine, and forest in White Park?"

Moses was sure they had searched everywhere a sane man would hole up in White Park, but these drygulchers did not qualify as rational, so he finally conceded and said, "I'll give the place another look."

"No you won't. Nobody's going near White Park before August 1."

"Pardon me?"

"I didn't have to tell you any of this. I've done so as a courtesy. The only man I have to answer to is Joshua Brand, whose instructions to you were to either help me or stay out of my way."

Moses' expression distorted his face. His breathing became ragged, like a bull seeing red. "If we can corral these butchers, we've got to do it! Right now!"

"All we have is a general idea of where they are. Odds are they'd spot our posse before we found them, and if they decided to pick us off we wouldn't stand a chance. Besides, they just suffered their first casualty, so they'll be chary. At the very least, a search now will drive them out of White Park and possibly Colorado, perhaps for good."

"I still say we've got to try!"

"And I say if you do try, I'll hog-tie you and toss you in one of your own cells."

Mudeater knuckle-rapped the chart. Glaring at

Kirk, he said, "Sheriff, what Paul is trying to explain is that a new search isn't necessary. Not so long as we have a good reason to believe that Hernandez and his crew will leave White Park come August 1."

"So you say."

"Paul and I have jawed about this quite a bit and we've come up with a strategy. We can post a dozen sentries at strategic locations around White Park on the morning of August 1. The less men standing watch for the least length of time gives the bushwhackers less opportunity of spotting us ahead of time. When they leave White Park, the lot of us close for the kill."

Moses disregarded that this sounded like a good plan. "What if the cross killers ain't in White Park? What if they're in New Mexico scrounging up a new Apache and decide to come back August 1 from the south?"

Kirk told Moses, "You know that Apache mercenaries are hard to find and twice as hard to hire. With August 1 only a few days away, they wouldn't have time. Go south and patrol the border for the bushwhackers, if you want. I have no quarrel with anyone taking precautions. If I'm wrong about White Park, Muddy and I will join you after August 1."

"I bet you will."

"Until August 1, however, White Park is off limits. If you don't like it, take it up with Josh."

Moses spent a lot of willpower stopping himself from tearing into Kirk. Likewise stopping himself from going off and confronting Joshua about

Kirk's demands. Moses knew Joshua would side with Kirk, but even if Brand surprised him, Kirk held the trump card. Moses could not begin to guess where Kirk and Mudeater's "strategic locations" were, and Kirk refused to reveal this information before July 31. So Kirk's threat to Long made sense.

Long asked Moses, "What are you doing, anyway?"

"Trying to work, Al."

The collier could take a hint. "All I wanted was some lunch. I'm going to the Galena."

"Maybe you ought to take a bath first?"

Long frowned at his hands and clothes and left.

Moses started to peruse the chart for the thousandth time, but decided it was futile. There was nothing on it that he did not already know about White Park, a primordial place if ever there was one: three fetid swamps surrounding hollows overgrown with rank grass, moss, creeping weeds, and monolithic trees, interspersed by gorges and canyons that in places plunged over two thousand feet. "Hang it!" he shouted.

Sheriffs were not supposed to sit around. Sheriffs were supposed to take action. Even more irritating, Kirk was right to wait. There was nowhere else left to search, and going to White Park now would only get a lot of men killed with probably nothing to show for the effort.

"Hang it," he repeated.

Rolling up the chart, Moses tried not to consider that he might be getting too old for sheriffing.

"I hope you know what you're doing, Kirk."

Moses heard footsteps. "Sheriff?" MacDonald entered.

"Yeah, Cully?"

"A fellow's at my office who rode his bicycle from Carson to deliver you a telegram."

"Are the wires down?" Moses always wanted to know immediately whenever that happened. One of the first moves renegades made before attacking any kind of settlement was to cut the telegraph lines.

"No, the wires are fine. This telegram came from Denver."

And the Nox office shared lines with the town. "Let me grab my hat."

CHAPTER EIGHTEEN

Penny was awake before she realized it.

She jerked, started to sit up, and felt two strong hands touch her shoulders and gently push her back down on a bed Penny found herself laying in.

"You lie still, child. Take it easy."

Penny looked around at what appeared to be an Ace-high hotel room until the smiling face of some middle-aged Negro woman eclipsed her view.

"Where am I?" Penny demanded. "Where's Papa? Where's Mama? What . . . ?"

The young woman suddenly remembered two gunshots, the attack, an Indian coming to help her, and then . . . that was all. There was nothing more to remember, leaving Penny with nothing else to do but wail.

"Oh, there, there, child." There was little else the Negro woman could say as she dipped a cloth into a basin of cool water sitting on the nightstand. She dabbed Penny's forehead, wiped away the young woman's tears, and repeated, "There, there," in a soothing sing-song voice as she ministered to Penny over the next several minutes.

When Penny's jag eventually subsided, the Negro woman got up and poured some clover tea into a cup. "Drink this, child. It will help your stomach."

Penny took a sip. "Where am I?"

"This town's called Eleanor."

"How'd I get here?"

Someone else in the room said, "I brought you, ma'am."

Penny noticed her Indian rescuer standing beside a chair, a Bible lying open on its seat. Scrutinizing the man a few seconds, she said, "I remember you."

"My name's Mudeater, though most folks call me Muddy. And this lovely lass is Miss Clarence." The Negro woman chuckled, flattered. "She strikes me as knowing more about medicine than most docs I've met. That's probably why the local saw-bones asked her to sit with you." Mudeater looked at the Negro woman. "How about I stay here while you tell Doc Gluzunov his patient's awake?"

"All right." Miss Clarence smiled at Penny again. "Can I tell the doc what your name is, child?"

"Oh. Yes, ma'am. I'm Penelope Fairchild. And most folks call me Penny."

"That's a lovely name. I'll be right back, Penny. Till then, Muddy will take good care of you."

"He already has, Miss Clarence."

Penny sipped a little more tea until the Negro

woman left the room, then told Mudeater, "Thank you for saving my life. I'm sure I'd be dead now if you hadn't come when you did."

"I wish I could have gotten there sooner, Miss Fairchild."

"Please don't. You did all you could." Another sip. "Now, what did you want to ask me?"

"Ask you?" Mudeater was taken aback. "How'd you know I wanted to ask you something?"

"Etiquette. Shouldn't you have fetched the doctor instead of Miss Clarence? I don't know you, and she was assigned to be my nurse."

Mudeater nodded his head and smirked. "You sound something like a friend of mine, Miss Fairchild. He's always figuring stuff out before anyone else in the room too."

"I'm a terminus dealer, Mr. Mudeater. Being observant is a part of my job."

"Well, that's true enough, I suppose." He picked up and closed the Bible and moved the chair to Penny's bedside. "Yes, I did want to talk to you. Alone. It's important, ma'am."

Penny tried to push as much of her grief aside as she could to concentrate. "Is something wrong?"

"There could be, but I don't think there has to be. You see, I wasn't completely honest with the sheriff—his name's Jeb Moses, by the way—when I told him about what happened to you and your folks."

"Why not?" Penny started to wonder if she should be worried about this man.

"Because, Miss Fairchild, I think it might be better for you if Sheriff Moses never found out the whole truth."

* * *

Joshua was reading a letter from General Palmer of the D&RG in regards to his and Ella's trip to Denver when Juanita entered the study. Speaking Spanish, she said, "Sheriff Moses is on the veranda, Señor Brand."

"Invite him in."

"He will not come in."

Joshua tried not to think about what had happened after the last time Juanita told him this. "Is he alone?"

"He is alone and angry. Very angry."

Joshua looked up and saw that she was quivering. *What now?* He went outside. "Jeb?"

"Hello, Josh," Moses replied, staring at the town, tableland, and mountains. He did not seem irate. If anything, Joshua thought he looked more at ease than at any time since Paul arrived.

"Juanita told me you were quite angry. You upset her."

"I'll tell her I'm sorry." He unpinned his badge. "Here."

"What are you doing?"

"Resigning. I'm resigning."

"Because you upset my housemaid?"

"No. Finding Jon's killers is the job for a sheriff, so why don't you make it official and give this badge to Kirk."

"You're talking nonsense! *You're* Eleanor's sheriff!"

"You lied to me, and I ain't laying my life on the line for anyone who doesn't trust me. Even you. I'll stay on until Teddy gets back from Denver. If you don't want to make Kirk your new man, you could do worse than my deputy."

"What's Coleman doing in Denver?"

Moses strolled off the veranda as Joshua called out about Coleman again. Stepping into King Charles' saddle, Moses trotted down the bluff as Ella rushed outside to find out why her husband was shouting.

"Jeb's quit."

"Why?"

Joshua opened the telegram to find out, and man and wife read together: *KIRK VISITED HIS FATHER MORNING OF HANGING. BRANDS KNOW. RETURN WITH MORE TOMORROW AFTERNOON.*

Ella wanted to faint. "Oh, good Lord! Coleman must have talked with Travis. It's the only way he could know."

"It'll be all right."

"It'll never be all right! If Coleman talked with Travis, nothing will ever be all right!"

"Yes, it will. This is my fault, and I'll make it right." He watched King Charles' trail dust drift into the air. "I swear to you I will find a way to make this right."

"Miss Fairchild?"

Kirk saw the tall flaxen woman with the dark brown eyes standing between her parents' caskets in K.V. Hadenfeldt & Son's Funeral Parlor, concentrating on a broach in her right hand. How long had it been since he had seen anyone as beautiful or so sad? She did not hear Kirk when he repeated her name, so he decided to wait. An hour went before Handenfeldt *père* entered and whispered to Penny. She nodded twice and shook her head once. Hadenfeldt thanked her and left, bidding "Good evening" to Kirk on his way out. She turned to see who was there.

He stood. "Good evening, Miss Fairchild. My name's Paul Kirk."

Did she know this hawk-faced man? She could not recollect. His name sounded . . . "Oh. You're Mr. Mudeater's friend."

"Yes, ma'am." He knew the pair had talked. Kirk had been grabbing a few winks after putting up the prefabricated house when Mudeater roused him for supper and to tell Kirk about Penelope Fairchild, including, "Those two people with her were her parents. She's with them now at the undertaker's." Kirk had made himself presentable and came directly to offer his condolences.

"I've been informed," she said, "that you are paying my expenses. I appreciate your charity, but I can't accept it."

"Oh? Well, of course that's up to you, ma'am. But would you please reconsider? On my honor, my only motive for wanting to help you is to make amends."

"For what?" The dried gutters on Penny's cheeks were beginning to itch. She wiped them away with the back of the hand clutching the broach. "I don't even know you."

"I was hired to find the men who waylaid your parents."

She stared straight at him, saying nothing.

"I hope you don't mind that I took the liberty of

erecting your house a few blocks from here on Powderhorn Street. You're welcome to stay at the Occidental for as long as you want. I thought you might like knowing your house is ready if you need it."

"Thank you." This man was a puzzlement to her. His clothes and arresting leathern appearance were evidence that Kirk was a frontiersman, but his manners, carriage, and choice of words were patterned upon a gentleman.

He asked, "Will you be returning east to bury your parents?"

"East?"

"I assumed from your accent that you are from New York."

"Yes, originally, but my parents loved the west. We've lived out here for several years, so Eleanor will suit them fine. Me, too, for the time being."

Without thinking, he told her he was glad to hear that.

She considered smiling, unsure why, but caught herself.

"My parents are buried here too. At St. Wenceslaus' churchyard, I mean," he said, anxious to move along.

"So are you, according to Mr. Mudeater." There was no irony in her voice.

"Sometimes Mr. Mudeater talks too much."

"Perhaps. He also said that I could ride the river with you, but I prefer to draw my own conclusions."

"You're wise. Why did he tell you that you could trust me?"

"He felt obligated to since you reasoned out that it was I who shot the Apache and not him."

Kirk turned to stone.

"He said that you knew from experience that he would have shot the Apache in the head instead of the heart."

"Miss Fairchild, is this a fit topic? I mean, considering?"

"It is. As I had the opportunity to tell Mr. Mudeater, I did everything in my power to avenge my parents, and shall be proud to tell the sheriff so after I'm finished here."

"Sheriff Moses may not understand."

"Not that it matters, but he will. I know from my experience that sheriffs like Jeb Moses tut-tut killings performed in self-defense. I'm sure he realizes that that Apache would have undoubtedly killed me if given the opportunity."

Kirk liked this woman's attitude. "May I accompany you to Sheriff Moses' office when you're ready? To offer any aid that I can then?"

"I would appreciate that. Thank you."

He sat, a patient man in less of a hurry than normal.

Penny looked back to the broach. "Mr. Hadenfeldt gave this to me earlier," she explained. "He had snips of my parents' hair put in it."

"That was kind of him."

"It was." She took a breath. "We use to sell broaches like this one in my parents store in Schenectady. That's where I was born. Even when I was quite young, I could remember us being very happy. Mama and Papa loved their work and their town and each other. I suppose Papa might have liked to have had a son, but he never seemed to prefer one over a daughter. He enjoyed teaching

me to hunt, to read and argue, and to fend for myself. Sometimes he'd say he taught me too well, but
I think I made both him and Mama proud. My
Mama was raised in Letcher County. That's rough
country. No place for greenhorns or a remittance
man, she would tell me. My mama knew numbers
and she knew herbs. She taught me about them
and about the womanly arts, games of chance,
how to deliver babies, to be loyal to family, and,
most of all, to be strong."

Penny appeared happy to reminisce about these
times, but now her expression saddened.

"I wasn't quite ten when Papa left us to go to
war. I bawled enough for two people that day.
Maybe I had to, since Mama refused to buckle
under to her tears. Mama was a realist about war,
and she had no intention of letting what could be
her husband's last glimpse of her be her crying.
She was too proud and too proud of Papa to permit that. As for Papa, he was so proud to be serving the Union. His pride in the cause never
wavered, even after he came home. But Papa had
changed. You've heard of Andersonville, haven't
you, Mr. Kirk?"

Kirk wiggled in his seat before he could stop
himself. Hoping Penny hadn't noticed, he said,
"Yes, ma'am."

"Andersonville has to assume some of the
blame for that change, but not all of it." Penny
told Kirk about Boston Corbett. "Papa just
seemed too itchy to stay in Schenectady after the
war. Maybe the town held too many memories of
the man he use to be. I don't know. Whatever the
reason, with Mama's blessings he packed up the

store, and before we knew it we were following the terminus circuit. We discovered that we loved being gypsies! Even so, Papa never stopped talking about the day he and Mama could finally settle down and I could attend school again. I'll never know why he wasted breath contemplating such foolishness. Papa only seemed happy when he was heading further west, and Mama and I were only too glad to accompany him. It was our life, and it was a good life for us."

Kirk, who had attended more than a few funerals, told her, "That's the finest eulogy I've ever heard."

"Was I eulogizing?" The woman gave Kirk a questioning glance. "I just thought I was talking." She looked at the caskets and tears returned. She laid her hands on each casket and bowed her head, tears falling onto the wood boxes below.

Detouring decorum, Kirk went to Penny. He put his arms around her and she did not resist. Patting her head, he said, "Listen to me. It won't be easy or quick, but you'll get through this, Miss Fairchild. You'll get through this. I know it. I promise. I do."

CHAPTER NINETEEN

The hands on the Waterbury clock approached one-thirty as Moses sat staring at a Beadle dime novel. He had not turned a page since before midnight when someone rapped on his front door. Die-hard reflexes got him armed. "Who's there?"

"Please let me in," someone whispered.

After the scene on Riffle Street, Moses was not taking any chances. "I said, 'Who's there?'"

Nervous seconds passed before someone murmured, "Ella Brand." Moses opened the door and saw a boy wearing a hickory shirt, Levis, and a tatty John B. The boy hopped inside and in Ella's voice asked, "Would you please close that door?"

"What in the world?" Moses turned up his kerosene lamp, an Argand-type that illuminated the entire room.

Ella tugged off her John B. "I couldn't risk being recognized."

"What do you think you're doing?"

"I'm asking you to rescind your resignation. Please. Joshua is beside himself and so am I. This town needs you. *We* need you."

"You needed Paul Kirk more. Make him sheriff."

Ella blinked. "I thought you were bigger than that."

"I'd be careful what you say while wearing those clothes. I might forget you're a woman and take a poke at you."

"And I might poke you back! This is more important than sore feelings."

"This has nothing to do with sore feelings!"

"Jebediah Moses, whatever Travis told Ted Coleman has nothing to do with your job, much less Joshua hiring my brother to help find the men who killed our son."

"*'Help'*? Listen, Ella, you started this. You were the one who warned me that your brother could be as dangerous as your father. Not that you've bothered to tell me why you think that."

Musing on that for a moment, Ella placed her hat on the table next to Moses' dime novel. "That's because Joshua and I have always believed that family matters should remain private, but if my word isn't good enough . . . if you think that knowing why is so important . . . I'll tell you."

Joshua stood at the front of the crumbling path leading to the Kirk's Victorian, eyeing the veranda, but didn't go up.

He just stared at the spot where the porch swing use to hang. Where he and Eleanor Kirk had rocked away so many enchanted dusks the summer Joshua turned sixteen. Until her father realized Joshua and Ella had fallen in love and Amos ripped it down by the screws.

At the time even Luther Brand could not figure out why his best friend railed against the romance. Today Amos' reasons no longer mattered, but the memories still haunted Joshua. Memories of Amos warning Joshua for two years to stay away from Ella, and memories of the letter Joshua received from Amos at Murfreesboro, written when Ella's father discovered that the young lovers had snuck off and gotten married before Joshua volunteered.

"I was right. You were an old fussbudget."

Joshua spat on the path, turned to walk away, but stopped when he thought he heard something. Maybe it was his imagination, maybe fate, but as a breath of wind gusted down the mountains, the man heard a familiar voice calling, "Josh!"

"Paul?"

For one whole second Joshua forgot all about Amos and the swing and even Murfreesboro as the ghost of a strawberry-blond boy, rail-thin, sprinted out the front door of the old gray house towards him. At the sight of twelve-year-old Paul Kirk, Joshua was ready to forsake all his cares and scoot off. Ready for fishing or swimming in Tansey Creek. Ready to run down the bluff on their way to the schoolhouse, laughing at poor little Eleanor as she bawled trying to keep up. Boys could be so cruel. Ready to search for arrowheads or fossils on the tableland. Ready to make a fort on one of the knolls outside of town and play Crockett and Bowie at the Alamo. Joshua was ready for any adventure . . . until Joshua remembered he was not twelve anymore. He was thirty-five, the year was 1879, and his son and heir, his pride and joy, was dead. Dead as Luther. Dead as Amos. And dead as his boyhood.

Ella was right about this place, he realized as he forced himself to walk away from young Paul's exuberant ghost. *It is full of painful memories, and all I've done is stir them up.*

Saddling Parbuckle, Joshua headed down the bluff. Intending to ride just long enough to clear his head so he could get some sleep, Joshua ended up going straight through town and past the southern hills. Joshua left the App by the gate to St. Wenceslaus' churchyard and, guided as much by memory as moonlight, found his way to his family's plot.

"Hello again, Father. I see you are getting some company."

Two open graves were waiting for the Fairchilds to arrive in the morning.

"It seems like I was just here asking your advice. A lot's happened since then. I suppose you know that. They say the dead know everything."

A waft tugged on his greatcoat, but Joshua noticed that the trees were not rustling and whispering like they should in the wind. Confused, he searched the faint crescent light until he spotted a dust devil kicking up grass and twigs at the foot of the open graves.

"More company."

Looking through the devil, Joshua could see the silhouette of Eleanor's southern hills, and recollected about another strange visit he had made here fourteen years ago.

* * *

"Paul," Ella told Moses, "came home in '65. Like Ted Coleman's telegram told you. Travis caught Paul talking through the window into our father's cell. If Travis was like Joshua, I imagine he didn't believe it was Paul at first. Not only because Paul was believed to be dead. Paul wasn't the same. The war was unkind to my brother. He was not the boy who ran off to volunteer in '62."

Joshua had not attended Amos' funeral, but felt obligated to pay some sort of last respects afterwards, especially since Ella refused to do so. He had tried to fight the impulse with a long ride, but in the end decided to go to the churchyard. In that day there were no school or Protestant church and the road from town was a couple of narrow wagon ruts. Even the churchyard's brick wall had not been built yet.

Riding over the hills, Joshua had spied someone standing in front of Luther's tombstone. He could not clearly see who it was from over three-hundred yards away, but, somehow, Joshua was certain this stranger must be Paul Kirk.

Moses peeked out his window as he sipped some coffee and listened.

"Up until that moment Joshua honestly believed my brother was dead. The fact is Travis would have never told us about Paul visiting our father if Joshua hadn't confronted him after this incident in the churchyard."

"What did Josh do when he saw it was Kirk?"

* * *

Joshua observed Paul in front of the large bluish headstone for ten minutes. Twenty. Thirty.

What are you doing? You fall asleep? Why don't you leave?

Drawing his Sharps out of its saddle scabbard, Joshua laid on his stomach, legs forked, and took aim. Could he hit a target from this distance? He had in the past . . . but today? For certain?

"No," he sighed.

Was it Joshua's imagination, or did Paul cock his head a bit? As if Paul might have heard Joshua and was tilting an ear for a better listen?

You're featherheaded.

Joshua crawled to the churchyard, imitating the solider he had been a few weeks earlier. Taking position behind a patch of witch grass, and sweating like a raw steak on a sizzling grill, Joshua took aim between Paul's shoulders, emptying his stomach of air before he squeezed the trigger.

"That you, Josh?" Paul turned around. Smiled.

Joshua forced himself not to shiver.

Paul seemed pale despite a prairie sunburn. Always thin, now he was downright skinny. Certainly no more than one-hundred and fifty pounds, the weight loss probably to blame for making Paul's eyes look like they were too small for their sockets. To Joshua, Paul resembled an ancient Hebrew nabi after a vision of YHWH, someone lucky to be alive but not sure he was glad to have survived.

Where have you been, Paul? What did you see?

Paul glanced over his shoulder at the Brand

marker. "Sorry about your father. Word has it Paw killed him."

"Amos did."

"Hard to believe. They were the best of friends. All those years. Hard to believe."

"Who told you? I'd have heard if you showed up in town."

"Don't be so sure, Josh." Paul smiled again, then it was gone. "I heard some news about it over the grapevine telegraph. The rest Paw told me this morning."

"I don't believe that. If you'd visited Amos, Travis would have told me."

"Travis is as much my friend as yours. He caught me talking to Paw through the cell window, and decided to let me in so Paw and I could pray and say our farewells. Paw begged me to leave the territory after I finished my business in Eleanor. Just let everyone think I'm dead. Said it would be best for all. Travis heard Paw say this, so as far as he knows I rode out this morning."

"No one knows you're here?"

Another smile. "You thinking about killing me, Josh?"

Joshua did not say no.

"If everyone thinks I'm dead, then what crime is there in killing me? Right? None, I suppose, except Eleanor isn't the whole world."

Joshua's expression begged the question: "What does that mean?"

"The War Department knows I'm alive. They'd like me to re-enlist. I'm on hard-luck leave while I decide."

"Right," Joshua laughed. "Have you seen yourself? You're a chewed up rug of a man, not good for anything, even the Army."

"I might surprise you."

"I'll tell you what surprises me. That Amos wasted his breath on praying. Father Campbell taught us that folks have no use for prayer where your father's gone."

It was horrible to say, but it did the trick, fracturing Paul's icy veneer. "Careful, Josh. I'll only forgive so much out of friendship."

"Friendship? What friendship? Your father murdered my father!"

"My father never murdered anyone."

"Liar!"

Joshua fired.

Paul did not bother flinching as the bullet buzzed his ear. It ricocheted off the Brand's headstone, carving the gouge on the north maria.

"That's no way to pay your respects to Luther."

"Amos murdered my father!"

"Paw put his hand on our Bible and swore in God's name to Travis and I that he killed Luther in self-defense. Then he made Travis promise to keep it a secret. If it hadn't been Paw's last request, I doubt if Travis would have agreed."

"Why would Amos do that? Why didn't he try and save his neck?"

"Oh, you know why. Not that it matters now. What does is self-defense isn't murder."

"You're a filthy liar!"

Paul erupted as if hit by lightning. He tumbled underneath the Sharps, bounced up and grasped Joshua's shooting wrist and shoulder with both hands. Twisting hard in different directions, he dislocated Joshua's shoulder and drove Joshua's face into the earth.

Joshua hollered and dropped the rifle.

Paul picked it up and unloaded it.

"Risky," Moses commented. "Kirk must have figured Josh really wasn't going to shoot him."

Ella stared straight at Moses. "Joshua tells me he was, and I've never doubted him. Or blamed him. I've never confessed this to another soul—not even my husband—but, you see, I've always suspected Paul's 'business' included finishing what Amos started. To get me and Jon away from Joshua."

Joshua's shoulder felt like it had been stamp-branded. "Where . . . did you learn . . . to . . . do that?"

"A lot's happened since Murfreesboro. Getting stabbed in the back was only the beginning for me. Not that I believe you would have shot me just now. I have a deep, abiding faith that you can't kill me. You'll never know how much comfort that's given me these past three years."

"But you can kill me?"

Paul squatted, surly, but shook his head.

"Paul left right after that, and that was the last we saw my brother until Joshua sent for him."

"So he didn't try to take you and Jon away? Then your suspicions can't be right."

"Jeb, Paul isn't a stupid man. When Amos told me of his intention to take Jon and I away from

Joshua, I pledged to kill myself if he tried, and our father certainly must have mentioned this to Paul. Amos never seemed to believe me, but Paul knows I've never been one to bluff. It's not in my nature."

Moses knew Ella well enough to believe that. "But if your brother knows you ain't bluffing—"

"All he has to do is kill Joshua. That'll keep us apart, which is what Amos really wanted."

"Don't be addle!"

"It's only logical. Isn't Paul a logical man?"

"He is, but . . . Ella, you're getting carried away! Kirk could have killed Josh back in '65!"

"No, he couldn't. Travis would have hunted him down. All Paul could do was to wait for an opportunity. These ambushes have finally given him one. Think me rotten, call me muddled, Jeb, but I wouldn't be shocked to find out Paul killed Jon and made it look like a cross killing in hopes Joshua would ask for his help."

Moses thought that farfetched.

"I see. Well, I grew up with Paul, and I think it's possible, just as I suspect Paul is using that Fairchild girl."

"Using her how?"

"Paul's only being charitable to her so people will see him in a good light."

"From what I've seen he's acting more from a guilty conscience. I can't deny I'd do the same in his place. Can you?"

Ella picked up her hat. "So he's fooled you too. Like he's fooled everyone else. Even Joshua."

"Why would he do such a thing?"

"So you and this town will doubt he had anything to do with killing Joshua after that comes to pass." She tucked her black curls under her hat. "I told you what you wanted to know. Are you still quitting?"

Was he? "I'm beholden to Josh for giving me a chance when few others would, so I'll ponder it. I told him I'd at least stay on until Teddy gets back. That should be sometime this afternoon."

"Joshua is leaving on business come morning, and I'll be joining him in Denver in three days. Can't you agree to stay until our return? We'll all have cooler heads then."

Moses said he would let Ella know before she left.

"Fine. Good night to you then."

The dust devil was gone. Brand decided if he wanted to get an early start he had better move along too. Tomorrow was going to be a busy day. Places to be, promises to keep.

"Sleep well, Father."

In the saddle Brand twitched the App's reins and headed home. Behind him the churchyard lay quiet as an empty amphitheatre in the night.

CHAPTER TWENTY

Thunderheads rolled in over the churchyard as Father Myers concluded the Rite of Committal.

The town was well represented. Almost every citizen attended. Most had heard about Kirk's liberality regarding Penny, so they were not surprised to find him standing beside the unfortunate woman while Bartholomew and Kathryn Fairchild were laid to rest.

A few raindrops fell as the line of mourners presented their sympathies. There were many offers of home cooked meals and inquiries if Penny needed anything. A few mourners also complimented a flustered Kirk for how he was helping Penny.

Papa heard right. Eleanor is a fine town, the young woman thought as the progression passed by.

Mudeater brought up the end of the line as the priest scanned the clouds. Myers said, "I'll get the gravediggers. I don't like the look of that sky."

"No need, Father." Kirk removed his coat and rolled up his sleeve. "We'll see to it."

This was news to Mudeater. "We will?"

Penny rolled up the sleeves of her dress and told Mudeater, "Mr. Kirk meant he and I." She and Kirk picked up two shovels the diggers had left beside the graves' dump and set to work.

Mudeater liked what he saw, but Myers, who had never seen the like, asked, "Are you . . . I mean . . . wouldn't you rather someone else did that?"

"It isn't my first time, Father," Kirk confessed.

Penny said, "If my parents had died on the trail, this would have been my job. Why should it be different here?"

"I see. All right, then. Do you mind if I stay? Keep you company?"

Penny did not mind. "Perhaps the heavens will hold off on the rain if you stay, Father."

"You give me too much credit, Miss Fairchild."

For whatever reason, though, the rain waited until Kirk and Penny were walking into town. Then a steady shower fell that washed away the dirt from the couple's clothes and skin.

"The rain feels good," she said. "It feels right somehow."

"That it does, ma'am," Kirk agreed.

Penny spotted Moses sitting under the overhang in front of the jailhouse and waved for Kirk to follow her.

"Afternoon, Sheriff," Penny said as she stepped onto the sidewalk.

"Ain't you two the pair," he chuckled, standing. Then, remembering, "I hope the funeral went well, Miss Fairchild."

"Yes, thank you. We stopped here last night, but you weren't in."

"I'm sorry I missed you."

"I wanted to tell you that I am the person who shot the Apache who attacked my family. Not Mr. Mudeater."

"That so? You're a fine shot."

"Will you want to question or arrest me?"

"It's not my concern, ma'am."

"Of course it's your concern! You're the law."

"Just until my deputy returns from Denver today. You can tell him what you just told me."

Kirk asked, "You're resigning?"

"Yes."

"Why?"

"Teddy went to Denver to ask Travis Morgan some questions about you, your sister, and Josh Brand."

Kirk could figure out the rest, but not what it had to with Moses resigning.

Moses, meanwhile, had no intention of mentioning what Ella had confided to him. "Why keep a job if I'm not allowed to do it?"

"You still think searching White Park now is a better idea?"

"It doesn't matter what I think." Then he said to Penny, "I am truly sorry for your loss, Miss Fairchild. If I can be of any service, don't you hesitate. Just ask." Moses went into the jailhouse and closed the door.

"What was that about?" Penny asked.

Kirk gazed north to the Brand house. "I wish I knew."

* * *

Where is Kirk going to put those sentries?

An annoyed Moses slapped the chart, wondering how it and his memory could both be failing him. There was no way he could see or think of to properly post any less than a hundred watchmen around White Park.

"A 'dozen' sentries? It can't be done. Kirk must be bluffing."

Why?

"This ain't your problem, Jebediah."

Try as he might, though, Moses could not make himself believe that. He could quit being sheriff, but he knew he could not quit hunting the cross killers.

As soon as Coleman got back and Eleanor had a lawman to watch over her, Moses would be free to pursue this matter as he saw fit. He might head south, like he suggested to Kirk, but not before making a cautious reconnoiter of White Park.

"Hang it; where is Teddy, anyway?"

The time was a quarter to eight and Moses had estimated Coleman would be back no later than dinner time.

Moses stepped outside. The rain was finally tapering in town. *But look at them clouds. It must be raining to beat the Dutch out on the tableland and up in the higher elevations.*

That should not matter. Coleman had traveled in worse weather.

Horses can slip in the mud. Mountain lions will prowl day or night in all kinds of weather. And Colorow's Utes haven't gotten any more peaceable.

"Teddy's all right. It's a hard ride from Lake City."

That it is.

Moses went inside to grab his slicker and a Henry. Saddling King Charles, he rode south. Galloping past the churchyard, Moses scanned the tableland but saw no sign of Coleman.

Teddy could have stayed in Lake City. Maybe there's flooding between here and there.

If so, Coleman would have telegraphed and let Moses know.

Maybe the wires are down.

If so, MacDonald would have . . .

This is nonsense! Teddy can take care of himself!

Moses dug his heels into King Charles' shanks, charging further into the tempest.

Kirk watched the storm from the playroom's window.

Since his sleeping in here was no longer a secret, he had removed the planks outside the window and stacked them in an empty corner. From here Kirk could enjoy following the majesty of the humbling cumulonimbus clouds migrating east in the darkling sky, spewing lightning and cawing thunder over the Rockies. He could also see a single light burning next door in a second story window.

Before the Fairchilds' funeral, Penny had read the Kirks' gravestone and asked, "Why won't you make amends with your sister?" He had told her Ella would have none of it. "That makes no sense. I would give anything to be with any of my family again."

Kirk had not wanted to trouble Penny with his

problems on such a difficult day. "I'm sure Ella would give anything to have her son back."

"Of course she would, but she still has you."

Kirk glanced at his mother's rocker. "I've learned the hard way," he had told Penny, "that people don't always make sense."

He looked back at the sky, but try as he might, Kirk could not ignore the solitary light next door. As long as it burned, he would never be able to concentrate on anything as pleasant as a thunderstorm.

"So be it, Ella."

He gave up and shut the window.

Moses found Coleman facedown beside a winding horseback trail south of the North Star Sultan Mine. Coleman's horse was sheltering under a piñon, waiting for its rider to get back on so they could leave. Dropping to his knees, Moses rolled the young man over.

Wiping mud away from Coleman's face, he found the bullet hole.

Tearing open the young man's shirt, he found an **X**.

The storm pelted the mountains as the old outlaw moaned like a lost soul, nestling Coleman's head in his lap, now knowing exactly how the Brands felt the day he brought their dead son home to them.

CHAPTER TWENTY-ONE

Ella found Moses brooding in Gluzunov's waiting room. The old doctor had insisted on examining Coleman's body alone.

She shook off her slicker and sat next to Moses. Things stayed quiet between them until they heard someone in the consulting room speaking to Gluzunov. For a hare-brained instant Moses hoped Coleman was somehow alive, but Ella recognized the visitor's voice: Paul.

Moses busted into the consulting room. Coleman lay stretched out on the examining table, chest exposed so Gluzunov and Kirk, standing across from one another, could study the X. A door leading into the alley behind Gluzunov's office stood open, neither man minding the rain. Moses snorted, "What are you doing here?"

"I'm sorry about your deputy, Sher—"

"*What are you doing here?*"

Kirk noticed Ella behind Moses. "What I came here to do."

"How'd you know Teddy was dead?" Moses asked.

"Bad news spreads even at this time of night. I heard about it while I was getting coffee at the Telluride."

"Coffee? You were drinking coffee on Riffle Street?"

"Yes."

"While those butchers are roaming free? Look what your waiting did now!"

"Those butchers had nothing to do with your deputy's murder."

Moses couldn't believe he heard Kirk right. "What did you say?"

Gluzunov told him, "Paul is correct, Sheriff."

"That's their **X**, Doc!"

"This bullet fired much closer to deputy than the others. Bullet hole smaller, though not much."

"Who cares about how big the bullet hole is? And it's been raining all day! Even these sharp-shooters couldn't see to plug poor Teddy from a couple hundred yards away in the rain!"

"Knife wound is also different."

"How? I know what an **X** looks like."

"Blade thinner. A Bowie, I think. Other incisions were thicker, like from kukri. These also not so deep. And they are jagged. It was difficult for this person to cut pectoralis major and minor. This killer not as strong."

"Then the big fellow Mudeater saw must have carved the rest. If that was Pedro, he used to tote a large Chevalier California knife. One of the two smaller men Mudeater spotted must have done this job."

"Why?" Kirk asked. "Why change what they've been doing? And why did they lay in wait where you found the deputy? It's miles from White Park on a trail even a tenderfoot avoids in weather like this."

"Their Apache got killed yesterday. People don't act normal when it comes to an eye for an eye."

"That Apache was a mercenary. Why would the other bushwhackers want retribution?"

The Pedro Hernandez Moses knew would not, but Moses did not want to be bothered about that. "Maybe they got real chummy the last three years."

"Sheriff, I can't ignore these inconsistencies. Neither should you."

"I'm not ignoring anything! I am going to find Teddy's killer, whoever it is!"

"Of course." Kirk glanced at Ella, said good night, and left through the alley door.

"Hold up!" Moses barked, following him. Gluzunov and Ella stayed inside, keeping witness from the door. Kirk's face and stance were slouched like a sleepwalker's as Moses asked, "How come you never told me you came back here to see your paw before he died?"

"It's none of your business. It's no one's business but mine."

"Is that all there is to it? Did you kill my deputy because Morgan could have told him something more than that?"

Kirk found that sadly funny. "Go ask Morgan."

"You have a reputation. Some folks even say you're a dangerous man."

"I'm only a devil," Kirk sneered, losing patience, "when it comes to outlaws. Just like you."

That tore it.

Lightning flashed as Moses feigned with his right. Kirk stepped back. Moses had seen this dodge on the Brand's veranda, expected it, and stepped in time with it to uppercut Kirk with his left as the lightning faded.

Landing on his shoulders, Kirk spat out blood and a tooth, his woozy mind wondering what business he had being conscious.

"Did you kill my deputy?" bellowed Moses. "I'll gladly beat the answer out of you if I have to!"

Kirk struggled to his feet and walked at Moses as if he had intentions.

Moses snapped off another punch.

Kirk blocked it and kicked out Moses' feet. "Go bury your deputy."

Moses threw mud in Kirk's face. As Kirk ducked his head, Moses swatted Kirk's left knee with the side of his fist.

Kirk howled as his knee bowed back.

Moses snared Kirk in a bear hug, hoping to crush the manhunter's ribs. The thin man's sinewy intercostals frustrated Moses as Kirk wiggled and kicked and punched, attacking spots that hurt Moses the worst until Moses had to release Kirk and retaliate.

Kirk managed to bend and twist enough so that Moses' punches never landed squarely, but they still hurt, and the clash came down to who could dole out and suffer the most punishment.

A punch to Moses' throat ended it. Moses collapsed as Kirk was about to do the same, both men bleeding and heaving.

Kirk couldn't talk; his jaw hurt too much. Moses was down, but he would live, so Kirk stumbled off.

Moses drew his revolver and huffed, "You answer me!"

Kirk peered over one shoulder and kept on walking. He had respected Moses despite their differences, but all deference faded from his eyes as he left the alley.

Moses dropped his revolver in the mud as Gluzunov and Ella came to help him back to the doctor's office. He had failed. Failed Teddy and Josh Brand. Failed with the cross killers, with Kirk, with sheriffing. He had failed at everything, and the worst part of it was, he knew he would never stop caring that he had failed.

Kirk recalled lumbering into the playroom and opening the window, but remembered nothing after that until the tangy smell of something sweet roused him.

There's light. Someone had lit a candle.

"He's awake." That was Mudeater's voice.

Followed by Penny's: "Let me soak this."

"Miss Fairchild?" Kirk started to sit up, then yowled. His ribs felt like they were lancing his spine.

"Just lay there, old son."

Penny asked Mudeater to remove Kirk's clothes to the waist. "I'll apply this hyssop to his face with a leaf poultice, but I need to wrap bandages around those ribs." She pulled wide dressings

from a pot simmering over a makeshift cook fire
burning on a marble slab borrowed from the
Kirks' kitchen. With Mudeater's assistance she applied the bandages and poultice, then inspected
Kirk's missing tooth. "A top bicuspid. No roots.
The tooth popped out clean, lucky for you. It
should heal on its own. I won't pack it." She
brought Kirk a cup of chamomile tea and told him
to drink it. It tasted like warm ginger pop and
made him feel a bit better. Drowsy too.

"I wish you'd . . . been the one working on me
at . . . Murfreesboro," Kirk regretted out loud as
his eyes closed.

Penny felt his forehead. "No fever. He needs rest
and time to heal."

Mudeater crouched beside Kirk. "He sure got
stomped. He's so skinned and bruised he looks
like the U.S. flag." He winked at Penny. "Thanks
for helping him."

"Thank you for bringing me."

"I wasn't sure what else to do when I found him
up here."

"You could have fetched Dr. Gluzunov."

"I figured Paul needed you more. He cares about
you, Miss Fairchild."

Penny's cheeks flushed. "You shouldn't con-
fuse care for kindness. Mr. Kirk told me he feels
obligated."

"Sure he does. So do I, but it never occurred to
me to help you bury your parents! Listen, I've
known Paul since '65. Seen him happy plenty of
times but only contented twice. The first was when
he got the telegram asking him to come here. He
was hoping it came from his sister. Of course he

didn't have time to waste on contentment or hope after he opened it and read his nephew had been bushwhacked."

She brushed red forelocks off Kirk's brow. "And the second time?"

"Today. While he was doing more than a man who just feels obligated would ever think to do."

"I see." She closed the window a little, then sat in the rocker. "What was that about Murfreesboro? Was he wounded in the war?"

"Uh-huh. Three Enfield bayonets right through his knapsack."

Penny sucked in air as if scalded.

"Him and his best friend, Josh Brand, only volunteered a few months before. They were with Shepherd's brigade when Sheridan ordered them to cover a retreat. Over five-hundred men were killed or wounded. The worst part of it, though, was Brand left Paul for dead."

"Oh." Penny had no more words.

"The Rebs' saw-bones patched him up, then they sent him to Salisbury. And in '62 Salisbury was a decent prison. Paul waited for his strength to return then escaped and rejoined the Union Army. That's when a general named Winfred Scott found out Paul was born in Richmond and had family there. Winfred Scott asked Paul to go to Richmond and collect information on the Confederates."

"He was a spy?"

"Paul doesn't like that word, ma'am, but he did a good enough job that, after the war, Allan Pinkerton asked Paul to join his detective agency."

"Is that where you two met?

Mudeater sealed his eyes. "No. That would be in Andersonville Prison. That's where the Rebs threw him after they got wise to what he was doing in Richmond."

Terrible tales told by her father scorched Penny's memory. "How long were you two there?"

"Too long."

"I am so sorry."

Mudeater caught a whiff of something more to Penny's sympathy than simple compassion, but did not pry. "Thanks."

Kirk mumbled in his sleep.

Mudeater stood. "Paul's going to be mad enough to eat the devil with his horns on when he hears I told you about all this."

"Should I keep it in confidence?"

"No, ma'am. Paul and I don't keep secrets, and I don't want you two to start. He does care about you, Miss Fairchild. As much as you care about him, I'm sure."

"Uh, Mr. Mudeater . . ."

"Sorry. I'm not good at pussyfooting, and I get the feeling you're not either. 'Sides, even an old fool like me can see you two get along."

For the second time Penny had no notion what to say.

"I love this stubborn gent like I would my own boy. He knows it. But a man like Paul needs more than a second father in his life." Mudeater picked up his bedroll where he had dropped it when he found Kirk earlier. "I'm going to beat the field mice out of a mattress in one of the bedrooms and get some sleep. That is, unless you want me to escort you back to town first."

Penny settled into the rocker. "I'll be fine right where I am, Mr. Mudeater."

That was what he figured. "Please, Miss Fairchild. Call me Muddy."

CHAPTER TWENTY-TWO

"Mr. Mudeater! Wake up! Please!"

Mudeater felt the world shaking. Penny was pumping the mattress, trying to rouse him. "Paul's gone!" she cried. "He went after the men who killed my parents!"

"What?" That served as cold water. "Is he *loco*? When?"

"I don't know! I woke up and found this beside me!" She pressed the Kirks' Bible and a water-stained piece of paper into Mudeater's chest. "He tucked that note for me inside."

Mudeater rubbed his eyes and read the note. "That sounds like Paul." Pulling up his galluses, he grabbed his shirt.

"Are you going after him?"

"You let Sheriff Moses know Paul's gone to White Park. Show him that note."

"The sheriff's resigned."

"Tell him!"

"Where should he meet you?"

Mudeater slipped his boots on. "He'll find me," then grabbed his hat and rig. "Get a move on, girl! For all we know, Paul's already dead!"

As Kirk slipped between lodgepole pines and yellow pine piñon, Douglas fir and blue spruce, he told himself that if he had a tomorrow, he would ask for Miss Penelope Fairchild's hand in marriage.

He had entered White Park an hour ago through the west swamp, careful to hug the dog birches so he would not get sucked under like a marsh pony in a mire. Since then he had cautiously trekked towards the heart of the park, marking his path with his knife in a way familiar to Mudeater but (he hoped) would go unnoticed by any bushwhacker. But Kirk had no delusions. He was walking to his own destruction and nothing could deter him.

Finding a brook, Kirk was careful to stop with a background behind him as he considered his next step. There was no way to cross without stepping into the open.

Listening to the wildlife and insects, all sounded right with the world, so Kirk rolled the dice. He traversed and ducked behind a clump of scrub oak on the other side. Loch Leven and cutthroats darted and grasshoppers jumped willy-nilly to get away from him, but a nearby flock of gray dippers seemed unconcerned. He was alone and safe.

Avoiding the most accessible and eliminating all but the nearly impossible paths, Kirk attempted to deduce the most likely difficult route through the park, confident this would be the way the bushwhackers would use to get to their camp. It was hard going, especially when burdened with the handicap of trying to remain out of sight.

Well into his fourth hour, Kirk had to keep reminding himself to focus on the job at hand and not let his thoughts stray. And his nagging left knee did not always make this easy. Finally something made Kirk's mind's eye blink: *Something's not proper here.*

Tracing his steps back a few paces, he noticed several conifer branches drooping a little too low so many months into summer. Warily brushing the branches aside, he found a stone wall constructed between a pair of mammoth boulders at the foot of a high rock face. At the bottom of the wall was a tunnel, passable only on hands and knees.

Kirk made one last mark by the boulders and then slithered through the tunnel.

He came out in a clearing of an uncharted river canyon. Red granite walls over five-hundred feet tall bordered both sides of the river's wooded banks, and in the wall across the river Kirk saw several caves carved into the granite by erosion. Kirk's ears pounded with blood. He was sure he had found Jon Brand's killers. He just could not see any of them, and that worried him. Like Kit Carson once said about Indians, "When you see them, be careful, and when you don't see them, be twice as careful."

A flock of gray dippers nesting along the river became motionless. *Did I make them do that?* The birds took flight as a flock. *Blast it!*

Not sure where the attack was going to come

from, Kirk twirled like a top, arm and knife extended, and managed to slash the forearm of a bandido stealing behind him. Assuming another bushwhacker would attack from the opposite direction, Kirk kept spinning as he drew his Army Colt with his free hand then dropped to one knee. The second bandido skidded to a stop less than five feet away. The manhunter stood and took three steps backwards so he could cover both men.

"Dónde's Hernandez?"

The ground beside Kirk's left boot exploded.

Kirk rolled and aimed up where he estimated the rifle shot had come. He spotted a massive man in a cave on the other side of the river, over two-hundred feet above the water, aiming a Sharps at him.

"My brothers and I are all Hernandez, Mr. Kirk. Please holster your weapon. I am too far away for your Colt, but as you've seen I can reach you."

Kirk holstered.

"Mátelo!" the bandido with the sliced forearm shouted.

"Not yet," the big man answered. "First we must find out if we can expect others."

"Go on and kill me," Kirk said in Spanish. "I am not going to tell you one way or the other."

Hernandez shot Kirk through the right thigh.

Kirk went down, gripping his leg.

"Suit yourself, Mr. Kirk."

Moses had no trouble following Mudeater's trail to White Park. He found the half-breed's unshod pinto ground-tied by the west swamp, along with Kirk's saddle but no grulla. That made Moses ponder if Kirk really was not planning on coming back as he gingerly dismounted King Charles, tugged his Henry from its scabbard, and entered the swamp.

Penny had insisted he read Kirk's note when she cornered him at home nursing his injuries and pride:

> *Dear Miss Fairchild,*
>   *Please give this Bible to Mudeater. He will know what to do with it.*
>   *I will never be able to repay you for the kindness you have shown me, or the strength you have demonstrated in light of such tragedy as has befallen you. However, like your brave father, I feel duty bound to try.*
>   *Make the most of life, ma'am. Never lose hope or faith. You, like Mudeater, are special.*
>   *Obediently yours,*
>   *Paul Kirk*

"Why would he go after them now? Alone?" Moses asked, trying not to care.

"Does that matter? Muddy said Paul may already be dead."

Moses thought that probable as he crossed the swamp, cursing himself for risking his neck this way.

On the other side of the swamp Moses found Mudeater's Sioux belt wrapped around the trunk of a young Douglas fir, cinched beneath a subtle horizontal scrape in the evergreen's bark. Moses searched and perceived the same scrape on another Douglas a few yards further into the park.

So long as you were looking for the scrape it was easy to spot, which Mudeater apparently wanted Moses to do. Loosening the belt, he stuffed it into a trouser pocket.

I guess it's as good a day as any to die, Jebediah, he thought.

One hour of hiking became two and threatened to turn into three. Try as he might, Moses could not help feeling a grudging respect for both the cross killers, for surviving in this verdant Avernus for months at a time, and for Kirk, if the man-hunter did manage to find the cross killer's lair.

"Huh?"

Moses heard a gunshot. Remote, but straight ahead.

Forgetting caution, Moses picked up his pace. Straining to hear any more shots, he glimpsed another scrape, realized Kirk's tracks doubled back here, and searched until he found the tunnel.

How'd he ever find . . . ?

Something or someone rushed from his right. Moses aimed at the blur, too late. A bandido with a gashed forearm was already past the Henry's barrel and driving a knife for Moses' gorge.

More movement. Mudeater, hiding on one of the boulders, fell on the bandido.

"Don't kill him!"

Mudeater rose, his knife blade red. "Too late. Now shush." He listened, as did Moses, who kept Mudeater covered. Nothing. "You here to help, Sheriff?"

"I'm here to end this."

Mudeater grinned. "You know, with those

bruises on your map, you and Paul could almost pass for brothers." He pointed to the apex of the rock face. "Can you get to the top of that?"

"Yes." Moses gave the face a second glance to make sure. "I can. Why?"

One . . . two . . . three . . .

Moses was counting to one hundred in his head. The Henry slung over his back in Mudeater's double scabbard, he pushed his stinging muscles and aching joints.

. . . seventeen . . . eighteen . . .

Mudeater was shimmying through the tunnel, likewise counting to one hundred. On one-oh-one he was going to come out its other end, more than likely where another bandido would be waiting to blast his head off.

. . . thirty-five . . . thirty-six . . . thirty-seven . . .

It was Moses' job to make sure that did not happen. He had to reach the top of the rock face then attend to any guard or guards standing at the tunnel's egress. After that, Moses and Mudeater were each on his own.

"I want Pedro alive. I've got questions for him," Moses had insisted to Mudeater before the half-breed slipped into the tunnel.

"That's up to him, isn't it? I want Paul alive. *If* he's still alive. That's all I care about."

. . . seventy-one . . . seventy-two . . .

Moses reached the apex as another gunshot echoed. Drawing the Henry, he limped down a steep decline. Moses skidded at the bottom, almost tumbling off, but kept his feet, righting himself at the brim of a cliff as drastic and dramatic as Cold Shiver Point.

. . . ninety-three . . . ninety-four . . . ninety-five . . .

He scanned the canyon. The egress must be on his right. It had to be. Counting *one hundred*, Moses prayed he was right, aimed that direction, and fired.

A bullet creased the stone by Moses' right toe. He threw himself backwards, hoping whoever had shot back would think they plugged him. A second round was fired, then a third.

Rolling to the cliff's brim and lifting his head, Moses gazed down. He saw narrow banks and trees, a clearing, a river, and a granite wall peppered with caverns across the water. Moses still could not see the egress or Mudeater through the treetops, but he did recognize Pedro Hernandez standing in a cavern parallel to him.

"Pedro!"

Hernandez aimed at the voice, but the brim blocked his view.

"Jeb Moses? That you?"

"Drop that Sharps, Pedro!"

"I can't shoot you if I do that."

"And I'll shoot you if you don't!"

"If my brothers don't kill you first. I got your man in the tunnel."

"And my man got the brother you had posted outside! 'Fess up! Your other brother and my man must have got each other with those last two shots or one of us would be dead by now! Just you and me are left, Pedro!"

"It's your life, Jeb. Your gamble."

"Yours too! Throw up the sponge! I'm in no

mood to try and wait each other out, and I don't want to kill you!"

"And there's no way I'm letting you leave this canyon. Go ahead and take your best shot. Better not miss. Once I spot exactly where you are, I'll bounce a bullet off that decline behind you to get you. Don't think I can't do it."

"Having first shot means the cards are stacked in my favor, Pedro. What do you say we both walk out of here alive? Throw down!"

"No. I like my odds, Jeb. I've seen you shoot! Hey, did you know that manhunter Kirk is still alive? We've got him tied up in that clearing."

"Don't feed me that, Pedro! I heard your Sharps twice on my way here. Kirk's dead!"

"I swear on *mi madre's* grave Kirk's alive. For now."

Moses believed him, but added, "Kirk is no concern of mine. This is between you and me. Since you won't throw down, I'm counting to three."

"Jeb!"

"You're grabbing the branding-iron by the hot end here, Pedro. If you don't drop your rifle by three, I'm doing like you said and taking my best shot."

"You try and I'll kill Kirk!"

"He won't mind. Not if it gives me more time to get you." Moses inhaled. "One." Exhaled and grabbed his hat. "Two."

Hernandez aimed where he best guessed Moses' head would appear.

"Three!"

Moses hurled his slouch hat into the air and sat up.

Hernandez trailed the sombrero's movement, saw what it was, brought the Sharps back down as Moses snapped off two shots.

One bullet pierced Hernandez's heart, the other his skull.

"Muddy! You hear me?"

The noise of Moses' gunshots rumbled over the river down the canyon.

"Muddy!"

"I'm here! Down here! Get down here!" Mudeater ran into the clearing waving his right arm. His left arm hung useless by his side.

"You shot?"

"I said get down here! Paul's tied up! And he's hurt bad!"

CHAPTER TWENTY-THREE

Gluzunov removed three bullets from the unconscious Kirk, all below the man's hips.

"Those varmints had him trussed up by his arms from a tree branch," Mudeater told the doctor after riding Kirk back to town. "Legs dangling."

Mudeater did not seem to care that he had been shot, left arm in a sling improvised from his Sioux belt. The second Hernandez brother had plugged him as Mudeater was about to escape the tunnel. "Moses saved my life, firing like he did. The brother shot at Moses and that messed up his aim when he heard me coming." Mudeater had shot back and his aim was dead on. "All I could do after that was keep in the tunnel and listen to Hernandez and Moses try to eucher each other. That big Pedro would have plugged me for sure if I didn't wait. When Moses counted three, I popped out to get Hernandez if Moses didn't."

"Good for you, you did not have to with that

arm." Gluzunov stared at the three slugs he removed from Kirk. "Same as bullets that kill Jon Brand and the others. All except Teddy Coleman."

"One of big Pedro's brothers must have shot the deputy. The brother who shot me had a Winchester carbine."

"Perhaps." He pointed to Mudeater's arm. "Can tell better after that one come out."

"Finish fixing Paul first, Doc. You can mine the lead from me after he's patched up."

Gluzunov waved a gory finger. "Your friend lost much blood. If that or wounds do not kill him, blood poisoning should. Even if he live, Paul Kirk shall not walk without crutches."

"One thing at a time, Doc." Mudeater stepped up to the examining table and laid a hand on Kirk's head. "He's got the constitution of an ox." But Mudeater knew that any man required something to live for in order to survive something like this. In the past Paul had been able to carry a hope that some day he would reconcile with Ella, and that had given him a reason to survive any adversity. Since coming back to Eleanor, however, Paul had confessed he doubted that was ever going to happen, and Mudeater was sure those doubts had influenced Paul's decision to set out early to White Park. Paul had sacrificed himself to find the men who had killed his nephew, trusting Mudeater and Moses would follow to finish the job. "You've got the temperament of an ox, too, old son."

"Should we notify Mrs. Brand?" asked Gluzunov.

"I suppose." Mudeater looked around. "Hasn't anyone told Miss Fairchild about this?"

"I don't know."

"I'd best find her."

Moses remained at the canyon after helping Mudeater get Kirk through the tunnel.

Climbing up to Hernandez's cavern, Moses admired his marksmanship before eyeing the big Mexican's Sharps. Putting it to his shoulder, Moses aimed across the river to where he had shot. Moses imagined Jon Brand walking through these sights. The Fairchilds. All of the cross killers' victims. All except Teddy. Try as he might, Moses could not imagine Teddy. Or would not.

Moses searched Hernandez's body until he found the Chevalier California knife. Moses unsheathed it and his imagination kicked in again. Moses did not like what he saw and threw the knife against a wall.

"I never pictured you for a coward, Pedro, but you never gave them poor souls a chance."

He rummaged through Hernandez's blankets, belongings, and, finally, saddle bags. "Wonder where you corralled your horses?" Moses hated thinking about the animals starving. "Got to remember to round them up." In one of the bags he found a small black notebook, binding cracked from frequent use. Moses opened it and skimmed the first page. He was rusty when it came to reading Spanish, but he remembered enough to make sense of this, and it made him sick.

"I take back what I said, Pedro. You're fouler than a coward."

* * *

The town was buzzing with news about the bush-whackers' demise as Moses rode in. Ned Scott caught sight of him. "Jeb!"

"Meet me at Doc's!"

"If you're checking on Kirk, he isn't there."

Moses pulled up. "Dead?"

"No. Well, not yet. Doc says blood poisoning will probably do him in, and Kirk's already running a fever."

"Oh." Moses felt an unexpected pang of sorrow. "Where is he?"

"On Powderhorn in that house he put up for Miss Fairchild. She had him moved there so she could tend to him."

"Okay. Then I'm going to see Cully."

"Jeb, I've got to talk to you!"

"Meet me there." In the telegraph office Moses told MacDonald, "Got to send a telegram to Lake City." Moses wanted it delivered to Joshua.

"I'm sure Mr. Brand is already on the way home."

"What are you talking about?" Ella had said her husband was going to Denver after leaving Lake City. "Why's he coming home?"

"Mrs. Brand wired him from the Nox building, right after that Mudeater brought Paul Kirk to the doc's office. She let him know you got the fellows that killed Jon. He wired back he was coming straight home. That was over two hours ago."

"All right. Thanks, Cully."

Scott caught Moses as Moses was getting back in the saddle. "You're leaving already?"

"What took you so long, Ned?"

"Come on, Jeb! You've got to tell me what went on out at White Park."

"Ask Mudeater. He likes to talk."

"Not right now, he doesn't. All he cares about is Kirk."

"Then you're out of luck, because all I care about it resting my bones a spell."

"Jeb! People need to know that the cross killers are dead! It's over!"

Is it? Moses wondered. "So tell them."

"But who were the cross killers? Was it Pedro Hernández? Why did they do it? Where is their hideout? Where are their bodies?"

Moses did not bother to listen as he headed home.

"Would Doc Gluzunov want you doing that?"

Penny applied another bloodroot poultice to another hole in Kirk's leg. "The doctor's left Paul's fate in God's hands. What he thinks doesn't matter." She sounded irritable, and made an irritable face at Mudeater. "Do you want me doing this? Or do you think Paul would want me to do nothing?"

Mudeater stared right back. "I trusted you last night. I trust you now. I already told you how I think Paul feels about you."

Penny walked to the stove where a tea made from bone-set and nettle was simmering in a pan. "All I can do is try and draw enough infection out of Paul's wounds to keep him alive. This tea should help ease his pain and maybe help break his fever, but to be honest, the doctor is correct. Paul's fate rests with God."

"And with Paul. He's survived more than a lot of men could in his life. He'll survive this."

Penny decided the tea needed to simmer some

more. She grabbed a cloth from a pot of ice water and draped it on Kirk's forehead.

"Ma'am, is there anything I can do for you?"

"Pardon?"

"Spell you while you get some air? Make you something to eat?"

"You cook?"

"Have to. Paul can't even grill a catfish. If I left it up to him, all we'd ever eat is berries and calamus."

Penny smiled. "After Paul's fever breaks."

"That could take a while."

"You must be starving. And exhausted." She handed him some nettle. "Here. That wound must pain you. Nibble on this, go eat, and get some rest." Her eyes were wide. "Let me do this."

Like I have a choice? he thought. "When I come back, I expect you to have done the same."

"Whatever you say."

You'd like me to believe that. "Fine then."

Penny turned the cool side of the cloth down on Kirk's forehead as Mudeater departed. Alone, she stared around her house. The Fairchilds' home. It looked the same, but felt utterly different.

"Nothing will ever be the same, will it?"

The fact her parents were not there to tell her it would was answer enough.

She watched Kirk, a man Penny had known for only two days. Why was she doing all this for him?

Am I just scared to be alone? Or to slow down and let myself mourn?

Fair questions. Even if the answer to both was yes, though, it did not change the fact that she felt something for Kirk. Something that could be strong and, she was sure, good.

Penny fetched her memory box and removed the note Kirk had written. Reading aloud, "I will never be able to repay you for the kindness you have shown me, or the strength you have demonstrated in light of such tragedy as has befallen you. However, like your brave father, I feel duty bound to try."

Kirk groaned and fidgeted. The infection was spreading. Even unconscious, he had to be suffering.

"I'll get that tea."

His eyelids fluttered. "Ella?"

You must hurt in so many different ways. "It's Penny. I'm here, and I won't leave you. Don't you leave me."

As she spoke Kirk ceased squirming, and almost, perhaps, smiled.

Brand arrived home late, but Ella was waiting up for him in the sitting room. Delighted to see his wife, he nevertheless told her, "You should be in bed."

"I couldn't sleep." She kissed him. "I'll never doubt you again. You said you'd find a way to make everything right. I couldn't believe it then, but you kept your word."

"Ella." He seized her. She felt so good. Brand had missed holding his wife. "Have you thanked Jeb?"

"No. I've been waiting for you. We can thank him tomorrow."

"All right. I bet he'll stay on as sheriff now that this is finally finished."

"Let's hope so. And we'll visit Jon's grave."

"Of course. What about Paul? Your telegram said he was nearly dead."

"That's the last I've heard."

"I'm sorry."

Ella kissed her husband again and whispered, "So long as you and I still have each other, Joshua, there's nothing to be sorry about."

"Bloodroot. Wonderful herb."

Gluzunov examined one of the used poultices. It was rank, brown, and full of sickness, like rancid fruit.

"Do you think Paul has a chance?" Penny asked.

"Of living? Always a chance, but even if he live he shall never . . ."

"One step at a time." Penny wiped her forehead with the back of a hand. She was tired and could use a good weep.

"The fever? You hear many of Paul Kirk's sins as it climbs?"

Penny had not expected that question. "Some. Rambling is to be expected."

"Yes. Nothing to make you think less of this man I hope. We all have our crosses."

"I'm not one to judge, doctor. After all, I am a terminus dealer."

"Really?" Gluzunov sounded delighted. "Then you have seen the bad in men."

"Paul's seen worse." Finished changing the poultices, Penny leaned back in her chair. "This is a good man."

The doctor approached her. "Little miss, time has come for you to rest. Go to that room in the Occidental. Tell them to ask Miss Clarence I ask her to relieve you." He put his hands on her shoulders. "I stay here until she come."

Penny's head went back and forth. "I can't leave Paul. I promised him I wouldn't."

"You are not leaving. You will return."

"That's not what I mean. He'll know if I'm not here and I can't do that to him."

Gluzunov was not heartless. "As you wish. At least eat. I have food sent over. Kirk will know if you do not take care of yourself. He will worry, and you do not want that."

Penny appreciated the originality of Gluzunov's argument. "No. I would not want that."

Travis Morgan came home feeling more tired than he had since the day he left Eleanor. Dora May, who greeted him at the door like always, could see something was amiss.

"Father?"

Morgan held out the latest edition of the *Denver Times*. "I just read some news from Eleanor, honey."

"Oh. I see." Dora May's eyes subtly brimmed with tears for a young man she'd barely known.

CHAPTER TWENTY-FOUR

Ella and Joshua Brand entered the sheriff's office, where Scott was pestering Moses. With the help of volunteers, Moses had just returned from White Park with the Hernandezes' bodies and horses.

"Thank you, Jeb," Joshua said, reaching out to shake Moses' hand.

Moses was polite. "You'd be better off thanking Kirk. This was all his doing, although why he went after the Hernandezes the way he did has me bamboozled."

"Perhaps," Ella suggested, remembering Moses' own words, "he was acting from a guilty conscience."

"I hope I'll get to ask him, but that don't sound likely. I am sorry, Ella."

Joshua asked if Moses had decided to stay on as sheriff.

"You're quitting?" Scott asked Moses.

Joshua said, "I hope not, Ned. This town needs Jeb." To Moses he professed, "I apologize if my hiring Paul ever made you think different."

Moses shook his head. "Hiring Kirk was a smart move. Like I say, you ought to be thanking him."

"Word around town is that you killed the cross killers' mastermind."

"Muddy killed Pedro's brothers. Took a bullet for his efforts."

Scott told the Brands, "I wish you folks had come along sooner. That's more than Jeb's told me since he got back yesterday. Wouldn't even let me ride out to White Park with him this morning."

"Ned, don't you have somewhere better you could be?" Moses snarled.

Scott could not think of anywhere.

"Jeb," Joshua said, "we're grateful you're not hurt. As much as we are that the cross killers have been brought to justice."

"All except one." Moses had preferred to discuss this without the newspaperman present, but maybe Scott's presence would help him keep his temper. Opening a desk drawer, he pulled out Hernandez's notebook and handed it to Joshua. "Found this in Pedro's saddle bags. You read Spanish, don't you?"

Joshua and Ella both did, as did Scott, who asked, "What is this?"

"A list. Pedro kept a record of every person he and his brothers killed."

"You're kidding!" Scott remembered something. "Good heavens! Kirk was right!"

"Right about what?"

"He said that the cross killers were behaving like merchants taking an inventory. They'd kill, check off a victim or victims with that **X**, then move on to the next."

Joshua growled, "That's exactly what Hernandez was doing."

Scott added, "He must have despised Coloradoans for that land grab."

Before either Brand could ask, "What land grab?" Moses pointed out, "Teddy's name ain't on Pedro's list."

The couple searched. "You're right," Ella said. "Hernandez must not have had time to note it."

"Pedro had plenty of time. My guess is he got most of the names for his list by reading the *Epitaph* and other newspapers, but he marked down what he knew—the whens and wheres—almost right away. Why else would the ink look different in the different columns?"

A grim Joshua told Moses, "You're stating to sound like Paul."

"A man's never too old to learn." Moses rubbed his bruises. "Maybe Ella told you, a couple of nights ago Kirk and I tussled after I asked him if he killed Teddy. I got it in my head that Kirk might not have wanted me to hear everything Morgan had told Teddy."

"What good would killing your deputy do when Morgan's still alive?"

"I wasn't thinking. I was mad. Upset. Now I've got it in my head that you might have been upset like that the night Teddy was murdered."

Scott was very happy he had decided to stay as Ella scolded Moses.

Moses ignored her and told Joshua, "You were on your way to Lake City that day. You could have waited for Teddy, shot him, and tried to make it look like the cross killers' work. Ella? You heard the doc and your brother. They tried to tell me somebody else might have killed Teddy besides the Hernandez brothers."

Joshua's face was crimson. "I did not see Coleman that day, Jeb."

"Ella told me you two were going to Denver after you left Lake City. Were you planning on dropping in on Morgan while you were there?"

"That's enough!"

" 'Enough'? Teddy's dead and the Hernandezes didn't kill him! I'll admit I was wrong about Kirk, so maybe I'm wrong about you!"

"Certainly you're wrong!"

"But what if I'm not?"

Joshua stepped to strike, but Ella put a hand on his wrist. "Don't. Jeb loved Coleman as much as we did Jon. And, as sheriff, he has the right and a duty to ask." She glared at Moses. "You are still sheriff, aren't you?"

Moses did not answer.

Joshua announced, "You won't be much longer if I have my way."

"Suits me. I don't intend to be wearing a badge when I catch Teddy's killer. And I will catch him."

Joshua and Moses gave each other bloody stares as Brand told Ella they were leaving. As the couple left, the husband warned Scott, "Print one word of this and I'll run you out of town! You'll think Bill Byers has had it easy when I'm through with you!"

When the Brands had gone, Moses said, "I'd do like he says."

"I know how to do my job. Are you sure he killed Teddy?"

"If I was sure, Josh would be in a cell."

"But you do think it's possible?"

"I wouldn't have brought it up if I didn't."

Something else popped into Scott's head. "You aren't going to quit, are you? The Brands are right, Jeb. This town needs you. Anyone will tell you so."

"Thanks, but one problem at a time. All right?"

Joshua said nothing as Ella laid flowers on their son's grave.

He spoke not a word during the ride home.

After he put away the buggy and stabled the horse, he sat on the veranda. Ella waited until dusk for her husband to calm down and come inside. When he did not, she went to him.

"Joshua, do me a favor?"

"What?"

"When I caught Paul in our old playroom, I noticed he had our family Bible. I'd always thought that Bible was lost. Paul no longer needs it. Would you retrieve it for me? It's probably on the seat of that old rocking chair."

Joshua reminded her that Paul was not dead yet.

"I know. But what if his Indian friend takes it or discards it? The man has no idea it means anything to me. Please? While there's still daylight?"

Joshua recognized this as a ploy to get his mind off his troubles, but, upset as he was, he was not going to refuse his wife anything at the moment.

He marched up the Kirks' front path to the veranda. Joshua peeked at where the old swing hung before entering the house, the front door's old planks standing where Ella left them. As he went upstairs he ignored haunting memories of young Josh Brand and Paul Kirk running down past him, shouting and pushing, puffed full of April energy and October mischief.

In the playroom Joshua found Lara Kirk's rocker, but the Bible as well as the rest of Paul's things were missing. Joshua double-checked but could find nothing. Assuming Paul took his belongings when he left for White Park, Joshua figured, *Moses probably has it*. Remembering Moses soured Joshua again and he left the house.

He found Mudeater outside, sitting on a front step, carving bites from an apple with an Arkansas toothpick.

"Evening, Mr. Brand. Care for some apple?" Mudeater pointed the knife at Joshua, a wedge skewed on its end.

"No, thanks." Joshua started down the steps, then stopped. "How's Paul?"

Mudeater smiled, glad Joshua asked. "Fever keeps climbing. He's tough, though. He's fighting."

"Paul's always been a fighter. I'd like you to know that I am grateful for what you two did. If Paul is unable to collect his five thousand fee, I'll see you get it."

Mudeater swallowed the wedge. "That's good of you. Could you give it to Miss Fairchild though? I'm sure Paul would want her to have it, times being what they are for her."

"Of course." Joshua started down again.

"That's where his plunder is. Over at Miss Fairchild's place."

Stopped again. "Excuse me?"

"I took his rig and other belongings over there yesterday. I figured you were here looking for them."

"No, but thank you."

This time Mudeater let Joshua get as far as the front path. "Well then, if you're searching for that letter Amos sent you, Paul doesn't have it."

"What letter?"

"The one you got in Murfreesboro right after Christmas '62."

Joshua went rigid.

Mudeater's eyes narrowed into slits. "Did you think Amos didn't tell Paul about that letter? Considering what you did to his son because of it?"

"So what is it you want? Something more than five thousand dollars?"

Mudeater stabbed the knife so its point buried in a step, laid his apple down, and rose to his feet. "If you weren't related to Paul . . ."

"You're the one who brought up Amos' letter for no other obvious reason than extortion."

"I don't keep or break confidences for profit."

"Then what do you want? What are you doing here?"

"Keeping out of Miss Fairchild's way and waiting for you to leave. I'm bunking here."

Joshua glared. What was this man up to? "Fine. If there's nothing else, good night to you then."

"And you."

Ella met Joshua at the front door. "What happened?"

"Your Bible is at the Fairchild home. I'll get it for you if Paul passes on."

" 'If'? Has there been any improvement?"

"Just the opposite, according to Mudeater."

"I see. Well, thank you for going over. I'll check on dinner."

Joshua watched her back. Should he tell her what Mudeater had said about Amos' letter? Upset her again, this time maybe for no reason? No. If Mudeater was going to blackmail the Brands the man would have tried tonight. Besides, if Mudeater ever did attempt to extort them, Joshua would attend to it.

Early on August 1, Kirk opened his eyes.

"Where . . . ?" His throat was dry.

Penny was there with water. "Your fever finally broke a few minutes ago." She was crying. "If you want, I'll tell Muddy you're awake."

Kirk caught her hand. Weak as he was, he still possessed a quick grip. "I heard you. Thank you."

"I haven't done anything."

One tear rolled down his cheek. "You've done more than you'll ever know."

CHAPTER TWENTY-FIVE

"Paul's going to live?" Ella sounded like she couldn't believe it.

"It'll be touch and go for a while," Moses qualified, "but it looks good. I was hoping you'd want to know."

"Why do you say that?"

"I remember what you told me. At the jailhouse and my home. But he's your brother, Ella. It's obvious he had nothing to do with Jon's killing, and, if you don't mind my saying, your suspicion about him has got to be wrong. I can't believe it's true after all he's done."

Ella screwed her head to glance down Juniper Street. She had been on her way to Cashman's Drug Store to purchase some Valerian when Moses called her name.

She regained her composure and, speaking softly, asked Moses, "Do you still suspect Joshua of killing your deputy?"

"I've got to consider it until I hear different from Morgan." Moses had telegraphed the Denver detective, requesting Morgan tell him everything Eleanor's former sheriff had confided to Coleman.

"Well, you have your suspicions, and I'll keep mine." She was still whispering, trying not to look as angry as she sounded.

Moses bobbed his head, disappointed. "Are you and Josh still planning on going to Denver soon?"

"Tomorrow. There's Nox business that needs attending."

"Could it wait until Morgan gets back to me?"

Ella breathed hard out her nostrils. "Why don't you take that up with Joshua? If you have the courage." She strolled away, pretending not to have a care in the world.

Penny sat near her open front door, bathing in the breeze while relaxing in her mother's rocking chair. Kirk was sleeping peacefully and, for the first time in days, she was starting to feel a little like her old self.

Almost dozing, the *rap-rap-rap* of approaching footsteps warned Penny to open her eyes.

"Oh Lord no."

She had never seen the woman with the black coiled hair who was coming down the sidewalk, but there was no mistaking the family resemblance.

Bartholomew's rifle was the closest weapon. Penny made sure it was loaded as she blocked the doorway.

"Good afternoon," Eleanor Brand greeted Penelope Fairchild.

Penny said nothing.

"I'm Paul's sister, Ella."

Still nothing.

"I'm here to see him."

"Please go."

Ella twitched, taking hold of her purse with both hands. "Excuse me?"

"Leave my home."

"Perhaps you haven't been informed. I own the land your house stands on."

"Take it up with Sheriff Moses."

Ella opened her purse. "I wanted to bring Paul . . ."

"Put your hand in that purse and I promise you won't live to pull it out."

Ella dipped in. "Please, I want . . ."

Penny worked the rifle's lever action.

"Why are you doing this?" Ella grabbed something tucked in among her cash.

Penny kept her promise.

Moses found a double-barrel Remington derringer clutched in Ella's hand inside the purse. That did not surprise him. Ella usually did carry a weapon whenever she was away from home. He searched the purse some more and found money and a folded piece of stationary. Unfolding the paper, he glimpsed Joshua's handwriting: *To my heart, I cannot apologize enough for the pain . . .* Moses stopped reading and folded the paper.

"She's heeled, all right," he told Penny, loud enough for a crowd congregating at the end of Powderhorn Street to hear. "Would you mind telling me, though, why you're so sure Ella was going to shoot you?"

Something about the expression that fluttered across Penny's face reminded Moses of *"Pinkerton policy"* as someone in the crowd yelled, "You're gonna arrest her, ain't you?"

Moses stared at Ella. She looked so much like Jon did when he first found the boy's body.

"Get Doc Gluzunov," Moses called back. "And I need somebody to watch Kirk until the doc gets here while I escort Miss Fairchild to the jailhouse."

CHAPTER TWENTY-SIX

Mudeater paced the Fairchilds' floor. "That woman is as stubborn as you are! I swear neither one of you'd move for a prairie fire!"

Kirk watched from the bed. "At least she can keep a secret."

"Don't try that with me, old son! I didn't tell Brand anything he didn't know already!"

"That's a fine hair you're splitting, Muddy."

"I thought you were ticketed for the misty beyond, and I didn't want you planted with people thinking wrong about you."

"That was my decision. You should have respected it."

"This has nothing to do with respect! This is about Penny! You never confided in her! She just happened to be here while you were out of your head!"

That was true. "Why won't she tell Moses what she heard?"

"Because she *cares* about you!"

"She's said that?"

"She doesn't have to anymore than you! People don't do what you two have been doing for each other unless they're moon-eyed! Now that girl needs you to save her life like she did yours. The mob around Moses' jailhouse ain't getting any smaller. Or quieter."

Kirk mumbled, "You're underestimating the people of Eleanor."

"Would these be the same folks who tried to string me up?"

"The vigilantes here don't lynch white women. Men like you and me, that's another matter."

Mudeater made a sour face. "Why are you risking this? Why wait at all?"

"I'm just trying to give Josh a chance to do the right thing. If he's kept Amos' letter and if he shows it to Judge Berthel, that will carry a lot more weight than my word alone."

"You've got your Bible. You can show the judge your family tree."

"I know!" Kirk took a breath. "I'm sorry, Muddy. Listen, if Josh doesn't act soon I'll get Moses down here. I'll tell him everything. I swear Penny won't suffer because of what Ella tried to do."

"She's got a noose hanging over her, Paul. The gal is already suffering."

Kirk could bust. This waiting was the hardest thing he had ever done. It was not like he owed Joshua anything.

"What would you do? Josh was once like a brother. Now he has an opportunity to make amends for letting me down when I needed him most. A chance that's come at the cost of his wife."

"Ella was your sister, too, don't forget."

"I told you before, Ella stopped wanting to be my sister years ago. I've got to accept that."

"You should have done that before you tried to get yourself killed at White Park!" Mudeater might never forgive Kirk for that jamboree.

Kirk looked at the northern bluff and the Brand house through a window. "Let Josh have until sundown." He looked at Mudeater. "Would you do different in my place?"

"I'm not in your place." Mudeater did not want to concede to Kirk, but he did. "I'll go explain this to Penny. Who knows? Maybe she'll understand."

"Thanks. And thank Penny for me."

"Do it yourself tonight."

Standing in his study, staring out a window and holding the note Moses had found in Ella's purse, Joshua tried to shut out the silence of his home. Juanita had been dismissed for the day, leaving him alone in the house.

Ella's funeral arrangements were completed, and Joshua had no interest in Nox business. He doubted he would ever be concerned about his family business again. Joshua did not want to live without his wife. If Jon were alive he would have a reason to go on, but his son's death only doubled Joshua's grief.

Everything he saw, everything his father had built and bequeathed, meant nothing to Joshua. "Why?" Brand would give it all away to have that answer.

He looked at the end of Powderhorn Street and the Fairchilds' prefabricated house.

"If you're looking for that letter Amos sent you, Paul doesn't have it."

"So what do you want?"

Joshua knew now. Mudeater had wanted people to know the truth about a friend the half-breed feared was dying. Mudeater could not tell anyone; Paul surely had told Mudeater about Amos' letter in confidence. On the other hand, it was not as if Mudeater had told Joshua anything that Brand had not known, and Joshua was under no such confidence to Paul. Brand was merely obligated by family loyalty.

"You could teach the devil a thing or two, Mudeater."

Joshua looked at the jailhouse where the Fairchild woman was being held and angry people were collecting.

She killed his wife. *She saved Paul's life.* Of both Joshua had no doubts.

"Why?" The question plagued him as his heart pounded with fury and dread. Pounded so hard that the blood thudded in his ears like gun blasts, and Joshua could not keep himself from imagining the shouts and wails of soldiers and, as he looked out on the tableland, picturing bitter Murfreesboro in December 1862.

As the Confederates burst through the Federal front, Brigadier General Sheridan, his ammunition supply exhausted, ordered retreat. The withdrawal created a gap, between the divisions of Major General Rousseau and Brigadier General Negley, which thousands of cadet gray coats and sky blue pants streamed through. Sheridan instructed Lieutenant Colonel Shepherd to cover the general withdrawal while the rest of Sheridan's forces readied to make a stand from a new position. Joshua and Paul's battalion, fighting with Shepherd's Fourth Brigade, was swiftly overwhelmed, but no man broke rank until Shepherd hollered, "Fall back!"

Joshua eluded the Rebs.

Paul was speared as he started to run.

And Joshua abandoned Amos Kirk's son without looking back. *"Three sabre bayonets in him! He must be dead! Must be! God, let him be dead!"*

Shutting his gray eyes, Joshua snatched a paperweight off his desk and flung it through the window.

"Why?"

It turned out that Joshua did know the answer. It lay in the safe in his bottom left-hand desk drawer. And Joshua knew what he had to do with it. And what it was going to cost him.

Looking at the southern hills of Eleanor, Joshua prayed, *Forgive me, Father. Forgive me, Ella. We have to do this. I have to.* "Please forgive me."

CHAPTER TWENTY-SEVEN

Four thousand residents surrounded Eleanor's blue ashlar courthouse under an uncompromising August sun, with two hundred more early birds crammed into Judge Virgil A. Berthel's sweltering courtroom.

Whenever something of interest occurred during Penny's trial, a snap of whispers commenced *largo* from the back benches, crescendoed to chatter as it was carried off to at last erupt *con brio* as loud cheers or jeers outside. Judging from the modulation of this babble, the residents were ultimately mixed in their opinions about this case. Penny possessed a lot of sympathy with Eleanor's citizens because of her parents. Almost as much as Ella Brand. To the benefit of all, the residents seemed to want to be certain justice was served instead of being overanxious for justice to be done.

Ned Scott could not have been happier despite the heat. He sat behind the defense table sandwiched between a frustrated Kirk in a wheelchair and Mudeater. So far Gluzunov, Moses, and five witnesses of Ella's shooting had testified for the prosecution. Penny's attorney, Wells Spicer, had asked few questions during cross-examination, but reserved the right to call back all of these witnesses. When the prosecution rested, Spicer asked his first witness to take the stand.

Joshua Brand swore to tell the truth, the whole truth, and nothing but, and Spicer asked, "Sir, do you believe your wife intended to shoot either the defendant or Paul Kirk?"

"Yes."

Berthel gaveled for quiet.

"Did she confide this intention to you?"

"No. Ella didn't leave our house that afternoon to do anything other than come to town on an errand. Sheriff Moses has testified that he was the one to inform Ella that her brother was going to survive his injuries."

"Yes, sir. Do you know why your wife would want to kill Mr. Kirk? Or how Miss Fairchild could have known this motive before she shot your wife?"

One corner of Joshua's mouth slid down in a sneer before he caught himself and leveled his lips. "Dr. Gluzunov already answered your second question during his testimony. Paul's fever made him delirious, and Miss Fairchild told the doctor the night before my wife died that Paul had been speaking secrets out loud."

"And what could Miss Fairchild have heard that would convince her she had to protect Paul Kirk from your wife?"

Joshua looked at the blank wall on his right. "You have to understand, Ella was more than self-conscious about how our peers view our family. She was exactly like my father in that way. I can't overemphasize how critical it is that you understand this about both of them."

"Why, Mr. Brand?"

Facing the court once more, Joshua closed his eyes, opened them, located Paul and locked his sites on the man. "My mother-in-law, Lara Kirk, was the daughter of a colored woman and herself an escaped slave."

Commotion lit through the crowd. Berthel gaveled, this time with the butt of his Colt, and when that did not work he put a hole in the ceiling. "One more outburst like that and I'll clear this court! Don't think I can't!"

Joshua continued. "I informed Sheriff Moses about this information and he attempted to find out if Miss Fairchild was already aware of it. This wasn't easy because she had no desire to break what she perceived to be a confidence with Paul. After Paul freed her of any obligation, she confessed to Moses what she knew about Lara Kirk's heritage."

Spicer turned to the jury, meeting their gaze. "Was this secret by itself enough reason for your wife to attempt murder?"

"It was good enough for my father." Joshua would have paid God to smite him then.

"Why do you say that?"

"My father tried to kill Amos Kirk when he learned the truth about Lara Kirk."

Berthel cut off another outburst by aiming towards the audience and cocking his Colt.

"Sir," Spicer suggested, "why don't you just tell us the whole story?"

Joshua could think of many reasons why not, but instead began with, "Amos disapproved of my romantic relationship with Ella. It was an attitude that I, Ella, my father, even Paul couldn't understand. Of course, Amos realized how my father would react if the truth about Ella's mother was discovered. Besides my father's concern for my family's social status, he was a vigilante and the furthest thing from an abolitionist. His father's farm would have been one of the first to fall if Gabriel Prosser's rebellion had been carried off.

"I never knew Lara Kirk. I was too young when she died. I saw daguerreotypes of her at the Kirk home while I was growing up. She was so light skinned that she had no trouble passing for a white woman.

"Amos cherished his wife. There was never another woman for him, and any honest man who remembers him will say the same. I know Lara Kirk's father was a widowed plantation owner in Edgecombe County, North Carolina, and her mother one of his house slaves. Given the daughter's parentage, she was educated better than the average slave. She escaped in 1838 and reached Richmond, where Amos was providing sanctuary in his home for runaways following the Underground Railroad. They fell in love, Amos completed her education, and the two were married. Amos quit Patrick Henry later that year under the pretense of wanting to see the frontier; actually, the couple was afraid, living so close to North

Carolina, that a visitor to Richmond might recognize Lara. My father, Amos' best friend, decided to join them."

"Where did you learn all this about Lara Kirk?"

"From a letter I received from Amos in December of 1862 that is now in Sheriff Moses' possession. Amos sent it after Ella confessed to him that she and I had married in secret before Paul and I left to join the war." Joshua glowered at Amos' son. Paul appeared to be drowsy, but Brand knew the man better than to fall for that act. "I've never figured out why Amos felt compelled to send me that letter. Maybe he thought I would stop loving Ella if I knew."

Joshua paused as Paul swiveled his head once to the right than the left.

"Whatever. When I returned home in '65, Amos decided to sell his half of the Nox to a rival syndicate without informing my father, his partner. He also told Ella he was taking her and our son, Jon, away with him whether she liked it or not. She was going to have none of that, but before Amos had the chance to try and follow through on his threat, my father confronted him in private. According to Paul, that was when Amos finally told my father about Lara Kirk."

"And that's when Amos Kirk killed Luther Brand?"

"In self-defense."

"Didn't Amos Kirk hang for murdering your father?"

Deep breath. "Amos preferred that to the alternative. The only way he could have exonerated himself was by telling the world his wife was an escaped slave, but that would have ruined Ella's life. He couldn't do that to his daughter."

"You know this for a fact?"

"Paul and I had the opportunity to talk after Amos was hanged. He said Amos made a confession to him and former Sheriff Travis Morgan that the killing was in self-defense. I didn't believe it then, but I should have. I've never known Paul to truly lie."

The prosecutor stood and objected. "What evidence does Mr. Brand have for what happened in private between Amos Kirk and his father besides Paul Kirk's word?"

Joshua told the prosecutor, "Ask Paul under oath. He has no reason not to corroborate now."

"Even so, sir, without evidence this is pure conjecture."

"I was asked if I believe my wife intended to murder her brother. I do and have explained why."

"'Murder'? There is no reason to believe your wife could even commit such a crime."

Forgive me, dear Ella. "There is. Ella was responsible for killing Deputy Ted Coleman and trying to make it look like the work of the Hernandez brothers."

This revelation stunned the crowd into silence.

Spicer approached the jury box as he asked Joshua, "And how do you know this?"

The witness leaned elbows on knees.

"Sir?"

Quietly, Joshua said, "My wife was a good woman."

Berthel almost called for a recess. "Joshua?"

"I can't ask anyone to forgive Ella. Nevertheless,

she was a good woman. She desired nothing more than to represent her family with dignity and class. Ella possessed both qualities."

"Joshua," Berthel repeated. "I appreciate how difficult this must . . ."

Brand held up one hand. "Don't."

If it was possible, the courtroom became quieter. Even Scott, who had been getting writer's cramp keeping up with Joshua, sat still.

"I know my wife killed Coleman because only two people had a reason to kill him the way he was found. Me and her. And I didn't do it." Joshua explained about Coleman's trip to Denver, the telegram the deputy sent Moses, and Hernandez's notebook. "Ella suspected Morgan told Coleman about Lara Kirk, and, according to a telegram Morgan recently sent Moses, she was correct. Not that it excuses what she did.

"Ella was at Gluzunov's office when the doctor and Paul informed Moses that someone other than the cross killers may have murdered Coleman. Someone weaker. Too weak to slice through Coleman's chest muscles without leaving jagged cuts. That wouldn't have been a problem for me. Paul knows that, and I don't doubt Ella was wise enough to figure out that her brother had probably deduced who the only logical suspect was on the spot. When Paul didn't die, she couldn't take the chance he'd tell Moses everything. As good a woman as she was, Ella never could understand that Paul would suffer anything before he hurt her. He loved his sister, even though Ella tried hard to convince him that the feeling was no longer mutual."

The prosecutor stood again. "Your honor, even if

all this conjecture is true, there is no way Mr. Brand can be certain that his wife killed Deputy Coleman, any more than he can be that she went to the Fairchild home to kill her brother."

Spicer started to counter, but Joshua cut him off. "I *know* all this is true because I know my wife! Do you think I would be sitting here shredding her memory if I wasn't convinced that this is the truth?"

"Your honor?"

"Overruled!" Berthel told Spicer to continue, but the defense attorney had no more questions.

Joshua left the stand, returned to his seat, and looked at no one for the remainder of the trial.

"Ella killed Teddy?" Scott marveled. "I never even considered it."

The jury wasted no time returning a verdict of not guilty. As the crowd escaped the boiling court-room, Spicer and the prosecutor chatted in front of Berthel's bench while Scott talked with Penny, Kirk, and Mudeater. Moses listened to the four from his seat. Joshua stood by a window, looking outside like someone waiting.

"I don't doubt she could have done it," Scott went on. "I remember how she won a Winchester repeater at the Independence Day sharpshooter contest my first year here in town." Congratulating Penny on the verdict again, he excused himself to interview the attorneys.

Moses walked up. "I'm glad this all worked out, ma'am."

"Thank you, Sheriff."

"Please call me Jeb." He eyed the manhunters. "So where do you two scoundrels go next? Or is it against Pinkerton policy to say?"

"I'm not going anywhere until I can walk on my own two feet," insisted Kirk.

"And I'm staying put until he does," Mudeater added.

"I figured it might be like that. Listen, Muddy, Josh and I talked, and I've decided to stay on here as sheriff. If you're looking for something steady while Kirk's mending, I need to find me a new deputy. You'd do me a service accepting."

Mudeater laughed. "I didn't see that one coming!"

"So no, eh?"

"You joshing? Only a fool passes up a chance to work with Jeb Moses." Mudeater held out his hand.

Moses grabbed it. "That's fine. Come on down to the jailhouse and I'll swear you in."

Paul, tired, grinned as the men left. " 'With.' I wonder who's going to end up working for who."

"You two manage," Penny said.

Joshua came over next, looking only at Paul.

Penny stepped back to let the former friends speak.

"So why do you think Amos did it?" Joshua asked.

"Did what?"

"This." Moses had returned Amos' letter. "Why did Amos have to write me? Everything would have been fine if he had just kept his secret to himself. Telling me makes no sense, especially after trying to keep Ella and I apart."

"It makes perfect sense."

"How?"

"He wrote you after he found out you and Ella were married."

Joshua waited.

"You were family. You had a right to know, and I guess Paw finally realized Ella and I should too. It must have worn on him, keeping a secret like that all those years. He never did cotton to lying."

Joshua put the letter in a pocket, then aimed his face at the floor. "I see."

"I'm sorry if that doesn't satisfy you."

"One more question. In the churchyard after Amos was hung? You could have killed me. I think you wanted to. Why didn't you?"

Paul shrugged. "Same answer. You're family."

"Was. Ella and Jon are dead, remember?" Joshua moved to go.

"Thank you. For what you did for Penny."

Penny also thanked Joshua.

Without looking back, Brand told Kirk, "Keep your thanks. Consider us square." He walked out of the courtroom.

Morgan strolled into one of Denver's most notorious gambling halls, the Arcade, around one-thirty the following morning.

Jim Moon, the proprietor, looked up from his newspaper. "Hey, Travis! Got time for a game of pool?" Moon was a burly roughneck with a fondness for white vests. He had no penchant for most lawmen, but was always glad to see Morgan.

"Not tonight, Jim. Just dropped by to see if your sports were behaving."

"No troubles tonight. See the *Times*?"

"Not yet."

"There was a big trial in your old town today."

"Yeah, I've been following that." Morgan still could not get over that little Ella was dead.

"The jury voted not guilty inside of half an hour."

"Is that right?"

"One of the dandies who owns the Nox syndicate got on the stand and cleared everything up."

"You mean Josh Brand?"

"You know him? Didn't do himself no favors, but he kept this Fairchild gal's neck out of the noose. John Shanssey in Fort Griffin told me about her once. She's a mighty fine dealer."

"What do you mean Josh didn't do himself any favors?" Morgan held out his hand for Moon's newspaper and started reading.

There it was. All of it and more, out in the open after so many years.

"See what I mean? As far as any near-do-wells will care, the name 'Brand' is mud, just like 'Kirk'."

"Oh, who cares what people think?" Morgan shook his head. Who could have seen things working out this way? "You know what, Jim? Life's too confounded short. Rack 'em up."

CHAPTER TWENTY-EIGHT

A chinook blew into the San Juans on New Year's 1880, blessing southwestern Colorado with a brief rest before another Rocky Mountain winter.

Paul Kirk, leaning on two canes, watched Penny Fairchild place evergreen boughs on the gravestones of both their parents, his sister, and nephew.

"I like to think that Joshua Brand will come back someday," Penny commented as she finished. "For his family, if no other reason."

Kirk kept his own counsel.

Joshua had departed Eleanor soon after Penny's trial, but not before seeing to his employees by talking Kirk into taking over the Nox. Not all the employees appreciated the change at first, but the situation was improving. Where Joshua went, or if the man ever planned to return, Kirk had no notion. As far as Kirk was concerned, Joshua Brand represented the past. Penny represented the future, and come the first day of spring Kirk intended to prove it by presenting her with a ring he had purchased through the Sears & Roebuck catalog.

Kirk took her hand. "Just don't you ever leave. Okay?"

"Don't you know by now that we can always depend on one another?"

Yes. He did.

Alongside a river running through an uncharted canyon, three graves with simple wooden crosses lay under the snow. Only a single word appears on each cross: "Bushwhacker."

GUNS
IN OREGON
LAURAN PAINE

Nobody ever ended up in Younger, Oregon, unless he had specific business there. Which was why Deputy Sheriff Jim Crawford was so suspicious when Edward Given rode into town. Folks had no idea why he was there, but they did know Given had the fastest draw they'd ever seen. And those skills came in mighty handy when a group of well-organized cowboys attacked their town and rode off with all the money in their safe. Now Crawford has no choice but to trust this stranger if he wants to catch the thieves. Yet the unlikely pair soon discovers that the robbery was just a cover for an even bigger operation—and that Given is not the only one in town with secrets.

Lonesome Range

JOHN D. NESBITT

Lyle McGavin is a very dangerous man. He's one of the most powerful land developers in the area, an overbearing bully who's used to having his own way and who's definitely not above using threats and physical harm to get what he wants or protect what's his. Too bad he has such an attractive wife. It's especially too bad for Lane Weller, a sometime ranch hand who's fallen in love with Cora McGavin. She says she loves him too, but she never should have left Lane's love letters where her jealous husband could find them…

#49
WILDERNESS
WOLVERINE
David Thompson

In the harsh wilderness of the Rocky Mountains, every day presents a new challenge. Nate King and his family have survived by overcoming those challenges, one by one. But in the new valley that is their home, they face perils they've never before known. Some of the most vicious predators on the continent are stalking the Kings and their friends. Nate has gone up against grizzlies, mountain lions, and enraged buffalo, but he's never battled wolverines—cunningly savage killers that know no fear. One wolverine is dangerous enough, but five live in this valley…and they're out for blood.

LOUIS L'AMOUR

A MAN CALLED TRENT

Louis L'Amour is one of the most popular, beloved and honored of all American authors. For many readers, his novels and stories have become the very definition of the Old West. Collected here are two of L'Amour's classic novellas, both featuring enigmatic gunfighter Lance Kilkenny. "The Rider of Lost Creek" was first published in a magazine as a novella, then, nearly thirty years later, expanded by L'Amour to novel length. This book presents, for the first time ever in paperback, the original version, as L'Amour first wrote it. "A Man Called Trent" was also written initially as a novella, only to be expanded many years later. Readers can once again enjoy it, restored to its original glory.

TIM McGUIRE

THE LAW OF THE BARBARY COAST

Clay Cole came to San Francisco looking for one thing: a certain beautiful red-haired singer. But the man known as the Rainmaker finds something else altogether—trouble. He hasn't been in the city for more than a few hours when he's tossed in a cell, then taken with no explanation to meet some powerful strangers with an unexpected proposition. They're looking for men who are good with a gun, men who can handle danger, and Clay clearly fits the bill. A battle is brewing over mining rights outside the city, and things are going to get rough pretty fast. It's a powder keg ready to blow, and Clay is about to experience firsthand...

The Law of the Barbary Coast

MAX BRAND®

THE GOLDEN CAT

John Jones has never courted trouble. But his partner Rourke seems to draw it in spades—like when he agrees to escort a group of tenderfoots to a remote hacienda in the Sierra Negra. First they have to get an ornery old invalid, his beautiful daughter, her dandied-up fiancé and the rest of their entourage over some of the roughest terrain in the country. Every day, they risk their hides to protect their party against the vicious bandits who roam the area. But as they journey on and the murder attempts continue, it appears the most dangerous enemy might just prove to be one of their own.
